Enos. Hitchcock

Diary of Enos Hitchcock

Enos. Hitchcock

Diary of Enos Hitchcock

ISBN/EAN: 9783337125707

Printed in Europe, USA, Canada, Australia, Japan

Cover: Foto ©Raphael Reischuk / pixelio.de

More available books at **www.hansebooks.com**

DIARY OF ENOS HITCHCOCK, D. D.,
A Chaplain in the Revolutionary Army.

WITH A MEMOIR.

Edited by William B. Weeden, formerly Captain Battery C,
First R. I. Light Artillery, and Chief of Artillery,
First Division, Fifth Corps, A. P.

MEMOIR.

Enos Hitchcock was born at Springfield, Mass., March 7th, in the year seventeen hundred and forty-four. If we would learn the defects of the system under which he was educated, we should study the ideal picture which he imagined and portrayed in after years for the training of a family.[1]

"The object of it (education) has been to teach *what to* "*think*, rather than, *how to think*. The end of education, is, "to unfold the latent powers of the human mind, direct them "to suitable objects, and strengthen them by exercise; it is "the art of preparing children for the duties of life."

He graduated at Harvard College in 1767. He probably began preaching very soon, studying theology with the clergymen whom he assisted, for we have the following certificate, dated Aug. 18, 1768, from the ministers of Cape Cod.

"These may certify, yᵗ Enos Hitchcock A. B. having by "public Preaching and private Conversation (Brother Green "interlines in a tremulous hand 'so far as we are acquainted') "given us yᵉ Subscribers (Ministers of yᵉ Gospel in yᵉ County "of Barnstable) Satisfaction as to his Qualifications for yᵉ "Gospel Ministry & of his good Disposition in that way to

[1] Memoirs of the Bloomgrove Family, 2 vols., by Enos Hitchcock, D. D., 1790, p. 15.

"Serve and promote ye Redeemers Kingdom; We recomend "him to ye Work, Nothing Doubting (if providence spare his "Life) but that he will be a Blessing in the Chh."

   Signed

Joseph Green Barnstable.	Isaiah Dunster of Harwich
Isaiah Lewis Wellfleet.	Caleb Upham Truro
Joseph Crocker Eastham.	Joseph Green Junr Garm^o
Edward Cheever Eastham.	Nathan Stone of Yarmouth :

Evidently, he was solidly trained for his future career, as this certificate of progress shows. In May in 1771 he became the colleague of the Rev. Mr. Chipman in the Second Church at Beverly, Mass.

He was dismissed and recommended from the Church at Truro March 21, 1771. He married Miss Achsah Jordan of Truro.

We know little of his early pastorate. He must have been a diligent student, for in his late years he developed an elegant and agreeable style. He subscribed to the *News Letter*, as the receipts show. Among the items of bills for supplying his family, there are generous quantities of rum, sugar and claret, with moderate portions of coffee. There is no direct evidence that he yielded to the common weakness of making verses, but the following among his manuscript documents probably was of his own composition :—

> "THE SAILORS NOTE FOR PRAYERS."
> "I ROBERT DOWDNEY, bound to Sea,
>   Desire you all to pray for me;
>   That I may have propitious Gales,
>   And be preserved from all Ails :
>   From sinking down in mighty Deep,
>   From too much work, and little Sleep,
>   From Spanish-Rogues, and all disasters
>   From wicked-Men, and Peevish Masters,
>   From Whip, and Cudgell, Kick, and Cuff,
>   From Knocks, and Blows and — that's enough."
> "For the *Royal American Magazine*."

The war of the Revolution began its fateful course. Mr. Hitchcock served during the year 1776, though there are no diaries for that year. The only traces of this service are in three certificates dated at Ticonderoga, Oct. 21, 24, 25, 1776, signed by colonels Ephraim Wheelock, Ruggles Woodbridge and Jonathan Reed. These certify to his service as chaplain in these several regiments from Aug 10, to Oct 25.

When Burgoyne's expedition was mustering in Canada, New England was deeply moved by the impending danger, and by the urgent need of the country for men and the means of warfare, recruits swarmed to Ticonderoga and the northern borders; among them Chaplain Hitchcock, whom we shall accompany in the pages of his diary. The feeling of the community and the inspiration of individuals will be better comprehended if we cite Mr. Hitchcock's own words in reply to the representatives of his parish, after some experience of campaigning and camp life.

"The committee addressed him, as follows, " Dear Sir It "gives us Enfinite Satisfaction, That so Favourable an oppor- "tunity offers It Selfe in which we can Express our minds to "a Gentleman of your known candore and Inginuity with "whom we have Had the Honour of Conversing with=& "Earnestly Hope By the Blessing of almighty God that we "Shall Live to See Eatch other in Perfect Helth and Inioy "that mutial Friendship that Contributes to the Hapiness of "all Sosiaty." . . . . and as we have the "Honour of aquaintting you By the Desire of the Parish= "with what they have Done for you Relitive to your Support, "For Carriing on the work of The ministry amongst us . " . . . at a meating of the twenty seventh of "Augst Last Held By agornment the Parish Voted that from "the Time you Return, To us to Preach amongst us you "Shall Receive after the Rate of Four hundred Pounds for "the Remainder of this Preasent year Sir we should Be glad "to hear from you the First opertunity we have Nothing New "to Enform you of your Family are all well and I thnke It is "a general Time of helth in your Parish But Time would fail "us to wright what our Inclinations Leads us To — in Short

"Sir our Harts are full and would over-flow in your Praise
"Did we not and only Beg Leave to add our Sencere wish for
"your Prosperity So we must Conclude and End with earnist
"Prears for you and Subscribe our Selves you Sencere Frinds
"The Committee"
"   Dated at the Precinct of John Low Salem and Beverly"
"   Sep^t the 5th 1778 .   .   "

Captain Low's rhetoric was somewhat ebullient, but he
made it clear that the parish of Beverly respected the Rev.
Mr. Hitchcock and respected themselves. The Chaplain replied in these words:

CAMP AT DANBURY Oct. 2nd 1778—

Dear Sir.

I receiv^d your very oblidging letter of Sep^t 5th, by Serg^t
Dodge; by which I was advised of the doings of the parish
respecting means of my subsistence with them; it gave me
peculiar satisfaction to find that I was not entirely forgotten,
by a people, for whom I have cultivated a sincere affection;
& in whose service I am willing to spend my Life. tho I have
stept aside, a little space, in the great emergencies of our
bleeding country; that, if possible, I might have some influence with my fellow-countrymen, either by precept or example, to remain firm & steadfast in the Defence & support of
their dear & Heavenborn Liberties; on which depends the
happiness of ages to come — of generations yet unborn.

There was a peradventure also, that I might, by my presence & admonitions, give some check to the dangerous growth
of Vice among our young people; who, I hope, will before
long, return to dwell with the multitude of their brethren in
civil life, & form no small part of the commonwealth. how
unhappy must it have been for such a number of promising
men to have lived amidst the many Temptations of an Army,
for several years, without any public appearance or form of
Religion? this would have rendered their return dangerous,
lest they infect the whole flock.

Whatever may have been the sentiments of some ; these weighty considerations have not been without their influence, in my conduct : & if the mite, I have, by my services, cast into the public Treasury, has had a desired effect ; that consideration rewards all my toil & sufferings.

The considerable advances, the parish has made towards my support, as it shews their affection for & attachment to me, so it affords great encouragement to me to return ; I hope, by leave of Providence, that happy period will ere long arrive — I must, for the present, beg their indulgence ; as an example of leaving the Army, at this critical juncture, might have a bad appearance & ill effect ; & is displeasing to the Gen¹, unless in cases of great urgency.

The campaign is drawing to a close ; &, probably, we shall march eastward soon, when I can, with much more propriety than now, obtain a recess from the army.

That the peace of God may keep yours, & the hearts of the people ; & preserve you blameless untill his coming—that we may all rejoice in his presence, being made happy in his favor — is the sincere wish & earnest prayer of —

Sir, your & their affectionate Friend

and Serv! E. H. . .

Cap! Jn° Low.

Preaching the gospel was a more important factor in the life of the army then than it is in modern times. Every opportunity was availed of, when direct military service would admit, to hold regular religious services. Sometimes two occasions are recorded for one Sunday.

These letters belong to a later period, but it seemed proper to consider them now, as their spirit pertains to the Burgoyne campaign. Mr. Hitchcock then served as chaplain to Patterson's Brigade of Massachusetts troops. In the diary there appears the account of the disastrous retreat from Ticonderoga. In the following list we perceive the losses of our chaplain and likewise an indication of the manner of living in camp at that time :—

Lost in Retreat from Ti=

Two Blankets — one pair of sheets — a double gown — 1 Coat, 1 Waistcoat — 1 pair Breeches — 1 do overhawls — 1 hat — 1 pair shoes — four pair Stockins — 1 Bible & Psalm Book, & several small volumes — ½ ℭ Sugar ¼ do Chocolate — ½ do Coffee — 15 Gallons best Rum — 5 do best Brandy — 1 dozen Nutmegs — 1 quart Stotons Elixir — 3 Bowls — one looking glass — 2 Beackers — 3 wine glasses — 2 Cups & saucers — 2 Knifes & forks — one large Spoon & a small do 1 pair saddle Baggs — &c.

Among the documents are many bills for supplies from the Quartermaster's Department of the Army and from the Massachusetts Board of War. The following is an example :—

The Revᵈ Mʳ Hitchcock bought of the Board of War	BOSTON January 30 1778		
Mo 23	2 pair Shoes .	16/6	£1.13 –
	1 pair Silk hose . .	—	1.16.8
	2 pair worsted do Nº 9 . .	6/2	.12.4
	5 yards wooling Cloth Nº 10	9/9	2. 8.9
	6 yards Flannel	5/6	1.13.–
	2 Linnen handkˢ . .	. 3/4	. 6.8
	4 oz Silk	. at 9/2	1.16.8
			£10. 7.1

Receᵈ payment THOMAS IVERS Cash

We do not know the causes which led to severing the relations with the parish at Beverly. He resigned the connection April 6, 1780.

This letter from President Stiles, about three months later, shows that the step was taken in the regular progress of the clergyman's mission :—

YALE COLLEGE July 12, 1780.

Reverend Sir

By a Letter of 3ᵈ Insᵗ Mʳ Baldwin informs me that you would willingly settle again in the Ministry, where the Providence of God might open a Door for your Usefulness. There are so many vacancies in the Chhs that you must soon have this — Opportunity present you for doing good. Last week a gentleman from Hartfd Chh was with me in quest of a Candidate, and he has engaged Mʳ Prudden. I shall not fail to recomend you, Sir, if applicⁿ should be made to me by a place I can think agreeable to you.

If you retire from the Army, I perceive it is in contemplation that Mʳ Barlow[1] should supply your Chaplaincy. He has not yet preached; altho' I believe he will soon ascend the Desk. He is a young Gentlema'n of Learning Sobriety & ten thousᵈ Excellencies. His merit in Poetry & the belles Lettres & in the Sciences in general is great — so great that the World I fear will never do him justice. How he may succede in preaching I dont Know, but his Sensibility & Amiableness of Manners must certainly recomend him.

I am Dear Sir
Your affectionate Brother in the Gospel.
EZRA STILES.

REV Mʳ HITCHCOCK

At intervals, when on leave of absence, Mr. Hitchcock had preached to the First Congregational Society in Providence, R. I. He was installed in that pastorate Oct. 1, 1783.

One diary of the parish life in the year 1784 exists — interleaved in an almanac published by Thomas. The incidents noted are generally of matters occurring in the parish, especially deaths and burials, and of the petty domestic affairs pertaining to any family. Occasionally something interests us now. He dined frequently at Governor Bowen's. On the thirteenth of March the river was opened, after having been closed by the ice for two months. In April, his daughter Achsah died at the age of eleven years. Rev. Joseph W.

---

[1] Joel Barlow, 6, 1758, was chaplain in the army, &c

Willard, president of Harvard College since Dec. 19, 1781, visited him often, and sometimes preached for him. He must be the " Rev Willard " occurring often in the correspondence from camp, as he was settled at Beverly in 1782.   When Mr. Hitchcock went to Newport for " General Election " he dined with Mr. Channing, and in Boston he dined with Governor Hancock May 26.   He was on intimate terms with President Manning of Brown University, and they often preached or lectured for each other.   The parsonage (the house on Benefit Street, at the head of Church Street, lately occupied by George Owen) was raised June 28, and it was finished and the family entered into possession on the last day of the year. An "exhibition" occurred at the College July 7.

The Congregationalists of that day were liberal in the rite of baptism.   On Sunday, Sept. 26, our pastor baptized *by immersion* William, the son of Colonel Nightingale.   Monday he dined with Colonel, and on Tuesday with Doctor Nightingale.   It was a season of rejoicing in that well-known family of the tuneful name.

From President Stiles' letter and various references in the diaries, we perceive a substantial intimacy and friendly intercourse between the families.   Mrs. Stiles came to visit the Hitchcocks on the last day of September, and "set for home" Oct. 27;   which was a fair sample of the genial hospitality prevailing in those fair days of Providence, unvexed by the locomotive whistle, and unfretted by the telephone bell.

After Mr. Hitchcock's work in the ministry and his patriotic service in the army, nothing interested him so much as the cause of education — the true development of the people, whether in the family or in the school.   He delivered a discourse on education at a meeting-house on the west side of the Providence River Nov. 16, 1785, which was printed, and bears the name of Enos Hitchcock, A. M.   His degree of D. D. was conferred by Brown University in 1788.   He was always active in promoting free public schools.   In July, 1791, he was on a committee with President Manning, Moses Brown, Jabez Bowen, and many prominent citizens, to forward this great enterprise.

At this time he was preparing his most elaborate literary work, the "Domestic Memoirs of the Bloomsgrove Family." [1] The distinguished Doctor Benjamin Rush, one of the most accomplished Americans of that period, gave his counsel, as appears in this letter. Our copy is in the handwriting of that excellent historical scholar, Doctor Charles W. Parsons:—

PHILADELPHIA 24th April 1789

Dear Sir

The Rev? Mr. Rodgers * put into my hands a letter, in which you request my opinion respecting a work you have prepared for the press upon the subject of domestic education. I can only say that I am highly pleased to find that subject taken up by a gentleman of your principles & character in the literary world. The plan which you have chosen for your work will be new in this country. This perhaps may ensure it a more general reception, & more extensive usefulness.

The account you have given of the work is so short, that I am not at liberty to approve, or disapprove of it. I shall only remark, that by making only two children, the objects of all the parental care and instruction of the two principal characters in your book, you will be precluded from recommending those virtues & manners which are necessary to render family society between brothers & sisters useful & agreeable.— Should you introduce five or six children (which are most common in all families than of two) you may inculcate many excellent lessons of fraternal respect from the youngest to the eldest,— of protection from the eldest to the youngest,— of

---

[1] In a Series of Letters to a respectable Citizen of Philadelphia. Containing sentiments on a Mode of Domestic Education, suited to the present state of Society, Government and Manners, in the United States of America; and on the Dignity and Importance of the Female Character. Interspersed with a Variety of interesting Anecdotes. By Enos Hitchcock, D. D., 2 Vols., Thomas and Andrews 1790.

The volume in possession of the Rhode Island Historical Society bears the inscription, "Mrs. Goddard (mother of Prof. Goddard) From her Friend and Humble Serv? The Author."

* [Probably Rev. William Rogers, B. U., 1769.]

delicacy, even in childhood, between the two sexes, and of affection, between them all. The rights of primogeniture so much esteemed among the Jews, I believe are founded in Nature & have their uses in every family. Where the eldest son or daughter is honored & preferred by parents, a family is never without goverment, in the absence of parents from home, and when these parents are removed by death, there is a foundation laid in the habits of the younger children for a continuance of subordination in a family,—a circumstance always essential to harmony and happiness.

In the management of my children, I have made two discoveries. 1! That it is as necessary to *reward* them for good, as it is to *punish* them for bad actions. Nay further—that rewards are of immense consequence in stimulating them to industry—virtue—and good manners. I was led to adopt this practice by contemplating the principles of action in man by which God governs his rational creatures. 2!y I have discovered that all corporal corrections for children above three or four years old are highly improper, and that *Solitude* is the most effectual punishment that can be contrived for them. I have used it for many years in my family with the greatest success. My Eldest Son who is now near 12 years old, has more than once begged me to flog him in preference to confining him. The duration of the confinement, & the disagreeable circumstances that are connected with it, are proportioned to the faults that are committed. I have in one instance confined my two eldest sons in separate rooms for two days. The impression which this punishment has left upon them, I believe will never wear away, nor do I think it will ever require to be repeated.

Too much cannot be said in favor of SOLITUDE as a means of reformation, which sh⁴ be the *only* end of *all* punishment. Men are wicked only from not thinking. "O! that they would *consider*," is the language of inspiration. A wheelbarrow — a whipping post — nay even a gibbet are all light punishments compared with letting a man's conscience loose upon him in solitude. Company, conversation, & even business are the opiates of the spirit of God, in the human heart.

For this reason a bad man should be left for some time without anything to employ his hands in his confinement.   Every *thought* should recoil fully upon *himself*.

If you can make any use of the hints that are contained in this letter, in your publication, you are welcome to them. They are founded in experience, as well as in nature, and if reduced to general practice, I am sure would be found to be very useful.

With great respect I am Dear Sir your humble fellow labourer in the presumptious business of making the world wiser & better, and your sincere friend, and

Well wisher
BENJ^N RUSH

P S: Permit me to object to the *title* of your book: "Domestic Education, accommodated to the present State of Society, manners &^c in america" will be more simple, and striking.   Your name *must* be prefixed to it.—Anonimous books do not succeed well in this country.

The REV^D MR ENOS HITCHCOCK
    at Providence, Rhode Island.

"Sanford & Merton," so important in forming the youth of England, inspired by the teachings of Rousseau, was written and published by Thomas Day in 1783.   It does not appear that our author had read it.   He studied Rousseau and criticizes him somewhat freely, though he sympathizes with his general purposes in education.   Lord Kames, whose "Loose Hints on Education" was published in 1781, was his safest guide.   Kames' precepts, being condemned as "irreligious" by the Scottish Church, were welcome to a progressive Calvinist of New England, stimulated by the American Revolution. Hitchcock condemns Locke, cites Thompson and Gay, and warmly commends the course of Vice-President John Adams, in supporting education.   The book is dedicated to Mrs. Washington with a very complimentary address.

The best part of the work is the evidence it affords of the

character of Doctor Hitchcock as a man, husband and father of a family. "He (the father) will never appear as an arbi- "trary ruler over them ; but as an affectionate and benevolent "patron. Influenced by the gentle spirit of Christianity, he "will banish from his breast all moroseness and peevishness, "which would embitter his own life, and render his family "unhappy."[1] The whole record of our author's life — meagre and broken as it is — indicates that this was a sincere and candid expression of the man's own effort in living. The book is not a good piece of literary art. Like so many writ- ings of sensible men, it just fails in its highest effect. The style is agreeable and often elegant. All the theories and attempted methods are wisely conceived. But the new educa- tion does not breathe and live. The puppets Osander and Rozella are waxy little prigs, illumined by the impossible virtues of adults.

Doctor Hitchcock's relations with Brown University were very close and influential, as he was one of the most active Fellows. Sept. 9, 1785, he was on committee with the President and John Brown in correspondence with David Howell, M. C., to obtain an allowance "for rents and for "damages done the Edifice while occupied by the public."[2] In 1791 he preached the sermon at the ordination of Tutor Flint as pastor of the Second Congregational Church in Hart- ford, and the discourse was published.

In this year Hitchcock, in common with the citizens of Rhode Island, met a great loss in the death of his friend and coworker, James Manning, occurring July 29.[3] He was made chairman of the committee with John Brown and George Benson to confer and condole with Mrs. Manning on the death of her "late worthy husband." The funeral ceremo- nies were held in College Hall July 30, and Doctor Hitchock preached the sermon.

In this main office of his profession he was distinguished, being an "excellent preacher," as the records say. Among his printed discourses were one on National Prosperity, from

---

[1] Domestic Memoirs I., 27.

[2] Brown University and Manning, Guild p. 419.   [3] Ibid., p. 495.

the *Farmer's Friend*, in 1793; on the death of Jonathan Gould, in 1793; on the dedication of meeting-house, in 1795; on the death of E. Fiske, 1799; and on the death of Washington. We shall annex a sermon preached at West Point, not as indicating the power of the preacher, but to show the method of the time.

Dr. Hitchcock published a catechism for children and an essay upon the Lord's Supper.

Our diarist, surviving his friend Manning twelve years, died Feb. 27, 1803. He bequeathed $2,500 for the support of the ministry in the First Congregational Society. When the present church was built, in 1816, the society placed a tablet on the wall, embodying their sense of gratitude to their "faithful pastor and munificent benefactor."

Though these scattered incidents are meagre, they suffice to portray a man of the Revolutionary time. He was a type of those Puritans, who walked with God in this world. Never forgetting his clerical mission or the priestly sanction, he was always a citizen; trying to mould this present life in preparation for a future, which was constant and actual to him. His ministry, lasting a score of years, left indelible marks. The parish had not been long organized when he took it in charge, and it became one of the most prominent and most influential institutions in our growing city. When the Unitarian movement occurred, it became a powerful unit in that body. When the Civil War struck home to the foundations of society in New England, the ministrations of our revolutionary chaplain bore direct fruit. Eighty-four men went out from the First Congregational Church; fifteen of these died from wounds or exposure. The list is somewhat remarkable in that forty-seven officers, viz., two Major Generals, three Brevet Brigadier Generals, six Colonels, four Majors, eleven Captains, nineteen Lieutenants, one Chaplain, and one Surgeon were included in the muster. Verily, the shepherd had trained and had led his flock in the ways of patriotic sacrifice. When the country labored in the agony of those fateful years, the children's children of those to whom Hitchcock had ministered offered themselves on one common altar.

The chaplain was larger than the soldier; the teacher and

minister larger than the chaplain ; and the man was largest of
all. If we were to put into one word the impressions derived
from these records, it would be, "fidelity to duty." He was
faithful, and he tried to make faithful those for whom he was
responsible.

A DEVOUT SOLDIER:

A SERMON PREACHED AT WEST POINT, JUNE 23, 1782;
AT PROVIDENCE, FEBRUARY 2, 1783.

There is an observation of long standing & worthy our
particular notice. "That since the necessities of mankind require various employments, whoever excells in his own province is worthy of praise. All men are not educated after the
same manner, nor have all the same talents. Those who are
deficient deserve our compassion & have a title to our assistance. All cannot be bred in the same place, nor to the same
employment ; but in all places and employments there arise,
at different times, such persons as do honor to their society,
which may raise envy in little souls, but are admired & cher-
ished by generous spirits."— Spet^r, Vol. 6, No. 432.

When we find examples of this kind carefully handed down
to us thro' a long succession of time, their names embalmed to
perpetual memory in the trusty page of history for faithfully
filling up their station, & by some qualifying virtue raised &
established their character — when I say, we find such instances,
it should excite in us an emulation to get possessed of the
same — & there is no condition, among the various ranks of
men, without an example of this kind, from the general in chief
thro' the various grades to the soldier.

The one I now have in view is applicable to the latter, & is
given to us in Acts x. 7., "A devout soldier."

Great and pompous characters usually fill us with admira-
tion, &, at unawares, steal from us a respectful attention, even
tho' the person was destitute of every private virtue, while

those who have moved in lower orbs, but filled their little circle with every usfull virtue, have passed scarcely noticed.

Alexander, stiled the great, has long been exalted as a great general—deified as the conquorer of the world, in carrying his conquests from Macedonia to Egypt—by invading, with un-provoked hostilities, cities & kingdoms, & turning peacefull countries into seas of blood, leaving the wretched widow & helpless orphan to bewail, in dismal strains, their miserable condition. His miletary atcheivements were great, but they were such as marked him as the murderer of mankind.

And while such a character is justly doomed to everlasting infamy, here is one written to eternal fame. How much more worthy of your attention & imitation was his character, who, in a small sphere, used all his abilities to no other purpose than the faithful discharge of his duty required. This was the case of the soldier of the Italian band I have just mentioned, the honorable testimony given of him, was that he was "a devout soldier."

This character can not belong to anyone who only feels some slight impression upon his mind of his obligation to the Deity —or if it breaks out into enthusiastic zeal & ends in idelness & neglect.

But a full conviction of the uncreated goodness & excellence of the supreme Being—& of our infinite obligation to love & obey him—the exercises of a mind thus impressed will be those of profound reverence for the divine Majesty, the warmest gratitude for his infinite benefits, & an unrepining submission to his will, & a steady endeavor to do all the duties & offices which arise from our particular station. This all goes into the composition of a devout character.

This is the only solid basis for the practice of virtue & the enjoyment of happiness.

And where this principle lies as the foundation of men's ac-tions, those subsequent virtues never will be wanting which happily conspire to form and dignify the character, & that which has the brightest assemblage of social virtues united to the greatest degree of moral goodness, is most worthy of imi-tation.

As filial piety is the first suitable exercise of the child to the parent & the only principle that can secure a uniform regard to the other members of the family, so piety or devoutness to God should be the main spring of all our pursuits. We should consider this as the first and strongest obligation upon us, & make it the leading feature of our character—the others will fall in of course. Love and reverence to God are duties so just & important that no character can be complete without them. Tho' a person may be distinguished by many usfull & excellent qualitics, tho' he may, in some respects, be entitled to great honor & respect, yet, if he is wanting in affection & reverence to his kind parent & benefactor, his character is essentially defective & all his boasted dignity greatly tarnished— the bubble of popular applause may soon burst & disappear, or the next turn of the wheel may plunge as deep in disgrace. We need not search ancient record for instances of this—they come within our own knowledge.

But whoever would fix his character on an immovable foundation, must unite the love he owes to the great disposer of all events to the service he does for his fellowmen. When his usfulness proceeds from this principle it will be steady & permanent, & his dignity rise on this sure ground, which will baffle all the assaults made upon it—in him will be verified that proverb, "He that walketh uprightly walketh surely," & does it appear a thing unreasonable or impracticable that we should act on principle of piety and devotedness to God? nay, can we not more easily follow the dictates of reason & conscience than oppose them? & no one opposes the will of the Deity but opposes the information of his own mind—he acts contrary to the dictates of conscience—but he who obeys the will of the Deity only follows inlightened reason & the voice of conscience.

Now if we wish to act with honor & fidelity in our stations amidst all the changes of life, if we desire to quit this stage triumphantly & leave a spotless character to speak for us when dead ; then we must settle down in our minds as a first principle, that as we are the rational offspring of God, we should in all our conduct have a primary regard to him, & next to his creatures. In doing this we are pursuing the road of honor, interest and happiness.

Under the influence of this principle we shall ever pursue the line of our duty, whatever our business or employment in life. As we stand equally related to the Deity & are equally accountable to him for the part we cut in this life, so, when animated by this consideration, we shall feel equally the obligation to discharge the duties of our own province; for it extends with the same force to one as to another, & is suited to influence in every station & condition in life, & who is governed most by it will be most steadily usfull, entitled to most honor & respect from men, best satisfied with himself & receive the highest approbation of him who is a "God of Knowledge."

It was this principle that actuated Cornelius, commander of the Italian band. "He was a devout man, & one that feared God with all his house, who gave much alms to the people, & prayed to God always." The Deity was the first object of his regard; and from thence flowed benevolence to men. He carefully walked before the people of his commune in the fear of God; not only avoided vice before them, but taught them, by example & probably by precept too, to regard the Deity as the primary object of love & reverence, & that this ought always to be a main spring of their actions.

Nor was so excellent an example without its good effect upon the troops under his command. The sacred historian is very particular in mentioning one whose piety and attention entitled him to the distinguishing epithet of *A devout soldier*.

Actuated by this principle he would of course be led to discharge every part of his duty faithfully, & in order to do this he must in the first instance understand his business, he must be acquainted with his profession, both the principles & practice of it; otherwise he will be in danger of committing such errors as will expose him to shame & the public to injury. The art miletary, like all other arts, is to be acquired only by industry and attention. To be unacquainted with the duties of our profession, or bunglers in it, is disgraceful indeed, & no character reads worse than that of a bad soldier, because great consequences depend on his skill & expertness.

Being acquainted with his duty, he applies diligently to the discharge of it. 'Tis the part of a good soldier ever to obey miletary commands with cheerfulness, & execute his orders with great punctuality & exactness—to be patient and persevering under the hardships & difficulties of his profession. He will never suffer himself to be led astray by the crafty designs of those who attempt to promote sedition & mutiny, nor ever betray the important trust reposed in him by deserting his colours. An army should always be a band of brothers who have entered into a close alliance with one another as well as allegiance to the public, & consider that their mutual safety depends on their adhering strictly to the principles of the compact they entered into to each other, & the whole to the public. Whoever betrays his trust to the public or the confidence you have placed in him, either by desertion or mutiny, is your worst enemy ; he disappoints your expectation, does all in his power to destroy the government & strength of the army, & exposes you to all the ill consequences of such conduct. He strikes at the very being of the army, & is virtually the murderer of it. Therefore your interest and safety strongly point out the necessity of your discovering any such execrable person, when known to you, that the designed injury may be prevented.

But courage is another thing which goes into the composition of a good soldier's character. All the heroes of the field in old time were called mighty men and valiant ; not so much because of their bodily force as because they were men of firm and resolute minds, animated by the martial fire, determined by the sense of duty. He will face danger with an undaunted firmness of mind, nor ever perfidiously desert his post, or basely decline the fierce encounter of the field.

These are the leading features of a good soldier's character, & all these must have belonged to the devout soldier of the Italian band. He sought to know his duty &, knowing, did it with cheerfulness—just and benevolent among his fellows, faithful to his trust, obedient to command, vigilant in duty, & brave in the field. He was all this upon principle, that is, he believed in the Deity & was actuated by a sense of moral obligation. His love to & reverence of his Maker animated him in the duties of his station.

And, pray, was this a blemish in his character, that he act upon this stable & uniform principle? Did it lessen his miletary virtues because he acted upon moral principles? or rather, did it not give lustre & dignity to them & fix his character upon a sure & permanent basis?

But, surely, in modern times this maxim is changed, & he who would be a good soldier must be a bad man — must forsake the ways of virtue, sink himself into intemperance, profaness and every vice. This is a very gloomy reflection indeed, that men must abandon that principle which alone can secure their fidelity & make them happy, in order to be good soldiers! The plain English of this idea is, that a man must renounce that principle which would prevent his becoming a deserter, a mutineer, a murderer, or falling into intemperance, profaness & every species of debauchery, to become a soldier! This would indeed add to the horrors of war, if to be soldiers men must class themselves with infernal spirits!

The present vicious state of our army affords a most melancholy consideration! It must appear so to every person of thought & reflection who considers the fatal tendency of vice upon society, & that when the minds of men are freed from the restraints of a moral nature the political safety is endangered — for surely he who can trifle in the most sportive manner with the Deity & disregard the very first law that is upon him (love and reverence to his Maker) can easily be brought to violate his obligations to men.

It affords a very gloomy prospect to see so many young persons who were the hope of their parents, & might have been the ornaments & pillars of their country, sink into vice & sensuality, lost, not only to a sense of virtue, but of common modesty & decency, giving themselves up to the foulest blasphemies, defying the God that made them, with oaths and curses abusing the hand which feeds them, sporting themselves with the name of the everlasting God & continually invoking the thunderbolt of wrath upon their guilty heads! But, you say, perhaps you have no meaning in all this, or that you are in sport! A pretty apology! Will you offer this to your Maker when you fly to him in the hour of trouble? will you plead it at the bar of his righteous judgment? No meaning! & so the vilest things become innocent because done without meaning. But if this was the case, how happens it that this want of meaning always produces that vulgar, unpolite, hacknied sound of profanity which does so much dishonor to the manners of our army? The tree is known by its fruit.

As to its being in sport, men must have arrived to a most horrid pitch of wickedness who can trifle with the great Governor of the universe, his perfections & government.

If you were governed by the principle which actuated the devout soldier there would be an end to all these vile practices which tarnish the character of an army otherwise so respectable. Your social & miletary virtues ought to derive stability & lustre from religion. To the distinguished character of a patriot & a soldier it should be your highest glory to add the more distinguished character of a virtuous, good, man—then you can quit this stage in the full blaze of honor & receive a crown of glory infinitely higher than ever adorned the head of the greatest conquoror.

DIARY.

1777.

April 8. Set from home.[1] Very hot. Dined Newall's, reached Waltham.

9. Lodged Revd Cushing. Set off about nine oclock; dined Hows Marlboro.

10. Lodged Baldwin's Shrewsbury — Arriv'd at Brookfield.

11. Received of Capt Greenleaf 60 Dollars to be sent to his wife—paid him ten for my share of Tickets No.

---

[1] On his preliminary journey to the station at Brookfield.

3014 & 3015.[1] —Officers set off for Ti— about Ten o,clock—Fair Day.

12. Innoculated[2] about 10 o,clock A. M. took mercurial pill in evening, pleasant

13. Sunday. Took physick before sun rise—pr^d for Rev. Ward Ps. 103, 19 & 122. 6 & on—rained P. M. in evening very fast—took pill.

14. Cold & windy—took pill

15. took powders in morning. Cold and windy took pill in evening.

16. Wrote to Mr. Shaw & Polley—weather moderated— took pill—paid Brother Moses 2£ LM.

17. took powders—rainy—took pill

18. took pill—

19. took physick—went to Hospital—

20. Sunday. Revd Fish pr^d at Mrs. Walker's—

21. fair Day—

22. Symptoms came on, very drowsy, took an emettick.

23. very poorly—but keep about—

24. began to break out— .

25. more pock—

26. more still—

27. Sunday. rainy—feel poorly—

28. pock begin to fill up—

29. very sore—but little rest—

30. began to turn—Sore throat.

May 1. Soreness abates—Day of public fasting.

2. eat boiled fowl—

3. eat fowl harshed over with Sallet—

4. Sunday. dined freely on boiled Chicken—

---

[1] This is only the beginning. The reader may be surprised as he discovers how often our examplary and devout clergyman bought Lottery Tickets. The custom prevailed at that time, and all classes participated in it freely. The states granted lotteries constantly for all sorts of enterprises, and the Continental Congress (Stiness, R. I. Hist. Tracts, 3, 45) raised money for the war by this means.

[2] This method for preventing small pox preceded Jenner's vaccination.

5. Came out of Hospital to Revd Ward's—

6.

7. visited at Capt. Keys's —rainy—

8. Revd Marsh & others came to be innoculated.

9. lowry, rained some

10. lowry

11. Sunday. Brookfield Revd Ward's, Matt. 16, 26, Is:
57, 21—Revd Fisk came from Hospital.

12. Pleasant Day.

13. very cold for season—

14. went to Worcester & returned, met with Col^o Littlefield, pleasant Day.

15. Set from Brookfield[1] 3 o,clock P. M. oated at Patterson's, Ware, reached Dwight's about dusk—pleasant
Day.

16. Lodged at Dwight's Belcherton wrote Home by Post,
rains, set of about ten—oated at whites 7 miles past
ferry between 3 & 4—dined at Lyman's Northampton—went to Mr. Brecks & Dr Hunts—

17. Lodged at Lyman's Northampton, set forward 6
o,clock breakfasted at Edward 5 miles—oated at
Pierces in Chesterfield 5 miles—dined at Agars
Worthington 5 m—reached Daniels's 3 m—Showers—bad Roads—good Land.

18. Sunday. Lodged at Daniels Worthington, pleasant
morning—set of about 7 o,clock reached Clarkes
about ten, 7 m. Gageboro, roads bad, Land good—
half after two o,clock reached Staffords 7 m, of New
Providence, Roads begin to be better, pass^d Hoosuck

---

[1] In his journey to the theatre of war, our chaplain, accompanied by
Colonel Littlefield, went through Ware and Northampton, taking a line
between the Boston and Albany and the Hoosac Tunnel routes. He
passed through Chesterfield and Worthington, thence near the Hoosac
Mountain. From Williamstown he turned northward by Pownal and
Bennington in the "York Government," now Vermont. Through Ru-
pert and Granville he rode on to Ticonderoga, between Lakes George
and Champlain.

Mountain, fine Land—at dusk reached Jones Hoosuck 7 m—fine Land, roads better—

19. go on, thro part of Williams Town to Pownal in yᵉ borders of York Gover!, oated Tracey's, 6 miles, 10
o,clock—Roads tolerable—Land good a pleasant
River—dined at Capᵗ Billings Benington 8 m—

20. Lodged at Fay's Benington 2 m—oated at Galutias in
Shaftsbury—dined at Cornfields in Allenston, 8
miles—oated at Frenchs, Manchester 7 m—

21. Lodged at Man lyˢ in Dorset 6 m—oated at Smiths
Ruport 5 m—dined at Latherbees Powlett 5 m, oated
at Hickbees 5 m—

22. Lodged at Corees in Granville 5 m—throw woods 5
m—oated at Grangers Skeene 4 m— reached Skeene
about 5 o,clock, roads very bad, put up at Averys—

23. Lodged at Averys, breakfasted at Capᵗ Wakines—Set
off from Skeene 10 o,clock, wind Contra, arrived at
Ticonderoga 6 P. M. fair Day.

24. Dined upon flowr puding & Venison Steak.

25. Sunday. Heard Mr. Cotton A. M. Mr. Plumb dined
with us upon roast & stewed Venison, 6 °Clock began
Service interrupted by the floating away of yᵉ Bridge,
very warm.

26. Generals Poor[1] & Patterson,[2] Colˢ Baldwin, Scamel,[3]
Wilkinson & Hays dined here. Pudding, Veal &c.

27. Rained in morning. Prayers omited—fair Day—

[1] Enoch Poor, of Andover, Mass., in the words of Washington, "had
every claim to the esteem of his country." He was appointed colonel
after the battle of Lexington, and brigadier-general February 21, 1777.

[2] John Patterson, of Berkshire, Mass., received the news of Lexington
at noon. At sunrise next morning his regiment of minute-men was on
the march to Cambridge. His commission as brigadier bears date February 21, 1777.

[3] Alexander Scammell, of Mendon, Mass., Colonel Third New Hampshire. He was wounded at Freeman's farm, and much commended for
conduct in the field. The fair-minded Gordon (II. 549) praises his coolness as well as his courage. He was mortally wounded at Yorktown.
He was beloved for his amiable qualities.

28. Wrote Home by a Marblehead man, very warm—
    receiv[d] Letter from Home 19 May—the Enemies
    fleet discovered a little below Split Rock—General
    Patterson supped with us upon fish—

29. Very warm, some Cannon heard down y[e] Lake—noth-
    ing further appears—

30. Went up to y[e] Landing to see Mr. Leach—not well—
    very hot—

31. Wrote Home by Parsons No. 2 & to Rev[d] Willard
    with a thirty Dollar Bill Cap[t]. Whitcombe[1] brings up
    an account y[t] y[e] Enemy are gone down y[e] Lake—
    very warm—

June 1. Sunday.   No Service A. M. dined at the Gen-
    erals[2]—Letters from General Gates inform of Col[o]
    Meigs[s] capturing 70 men on Long Island & destroy-
    ing some Stores also y[t] the Troops in Canada are
    going to the Southard — Divine Service at Six
    [o]Clock 1 Chron 19, 17, very warm.

2. Rained a little last Night, cleared of this morning
    pleasant, a cool Southerly wind—Went to the Land-
    ing P. M. Mr. Leach better—wrote Home No. 3, by
    a person going to Lynn—fair, pleasant Day—

3. Wrote Home by the Post No. 4, the Field officers sent
    a memorial of their grieviences to the general Court
    —Col[o] Brewer[3] & I wrote to the Rev[d] Mr. Foster—
    Showry—drank Tea at Col[o] Marshals[4]—

4. Receiv[d] of Paymaster twenty pounds— paid Col[o] Fran-

---

[1] Captain, afterward Major, Benjamin Whitcomb, of Connecticut, a
famous partisan officer (Rogers, Hadden, pp. 4-9, 42 n., etc.), the fruits of
whose scouting operations will frequently appear. General Gates spoke
of him as "a most usefull officer" (MS. in N. Y. Hist. Socy.   Rogers'
MS. Notes).   He was accordingly hated by the British and Tories.

[2] At Brigade Headquarters, General Patterson's, probably.

[3] Samuel Brewer, of Framingham, Mass., wounded at Bunker Hill, was
authorized to raise a regiment for service at Ticonderoga.   He was
Colonel Twelfth Massachusetts Continental Regiment, 1777-8.

[4] Thomas Marshall, of Boston, commanded the Tenth Massachusetts
Regiment.

cis[1] six pounds, my proportion of the Stores together
with 2^{lb} 8^s 6^d paid before; paid Col^o Littefield
2^{lb} 18^s 5^d Expenses on the Road paid Capt Porter
30 Dollars which I borrowed to send Home—cool
westerly wind—fair Day—a Pickeril sent us two feet
& ¾ long[2]—

5. Bought q$_r$ Venison at 9^S —Col^o Hale[3] dined with us
upon fish & a Venison Stake—officers of the Brigade
turn^d out to exercise agreable to orders—drank Tea
with Major Hull—Head ake—no Prayers—fair &
pleasant.

6. The morning opens very fine but we happened to lay in
Bed till almost Eight ^{o}Clock—slept very sound after
a fine Supper of Venison Stakes, this may seem
strange, but it cured my Head ake—fair & pleasant,
dined upon roast Venison Stuft—

7. A Soldier in Col^o Marshals Reg^t set on ye Gallows ½
an Hour & receiv^d 100 Stripes for enlisting twice &
deserting. Col^o Hays dined with us upon Venison
Soop &c fair & pleasant—Report of ye Capture of
ye Milford.

8. Sunday. Divine Service at ½ past ten A. M. Mr.
Plumb pr^d Exod: 15, 3, present Col^s Marshals—
Brewers & Francis's Reg^{ts}; at ½ Six P. M. pr^d myself Ps: 119: 115, fair and pleasant, but something
warm and dry—

9. Went fishing up east Crick—News from Canada—by

---

[1] Ebenezer Francis, of Beverly, Mass., commanded one of the fifteen
battalions which were assigned to Massachusetts by Congress Sept. 16,
1776. He was a gallant officer, respected alike by friend and foe. " No
officer so noticed for his military accomplishments and regular life as he
was."

[2] As our Chaplain was a fisherman himself, we must not scrutinize his
measurements too closely. Fish stories carry their own ethics in every
generation.

[3] Nathan Hale—not to be confounded with "the spy" of glorious
memory—was Colonel of Second New Hampshire. He was afterward
taken prisoner at Hubbardton, and his conduct there was much ques-
tioned. He died in captivity. His case is fully treated by Rogers in
appendix 15, *Hadden's Journal.*

two Frenchmen, y! Burgoine[1] arrived 10th of May without Troops—y! many of the Soldiers had died— the Hessians uneasy—500 French imprisoned for refusing to enlist—300 at Isle la Noix, 200 St Johns, a Reinforsment of 4000 expected—cloudy A. M. cleared of P. M.

10.   Wrote Home p! Post No. 5, & to Rev! Fisk—dined on Fish, fair & pleasant, purchased two tickets No⁵ 57111669 & 70 jointly with Cap! Greenleaf.[2]

11.   Radishes with breakfast—fine roast Beef for diner glorious news of Gen! Washington's gaining a compleat Victory over the Enemy at Bound Brook[3]—no particulars—fair pleasant Day—something dry—

[1] John Burgoyne, Colonel Sixteenth Dragoons, Major-General in the army and Lieutenant-General in America, commanded the expedition from Canada and finally surrendered at Saratoga his splendid little army. A brilliant and superficial officer, popular in court circles,—having made a successful dash of cavalry in Portugal,—he was sent to America, where so many military reputations acquired in Europe have been wrecked. He had neither the breadth of intelligence nor the character required for an important campaign. By comparison with the home government, he succeeded in Canada and New York, in that their conduct of the campaign was worse than his management. See Rogers, *Hadden's Journal*, pp. lxxx., 387.

[2] Captain Moses Greenleaf, of Newburyport, Mass., our parson's partner in the lottery business, was a gallant soldier. Commissioned as Lieutenant early in 1775, in December he was made Captain to raise a company for the Continental line. This was mustered in the Eleventh Massachusetts, under the splendid Ebenezer Francis. The company suffered severely in the hottest of the battle of Hubbardston. The brave Greenleaf was in many hot fights during the whole revolutionary struggle, yet never wounded. He was (MS. in Massachusetts Historical Society, Greenleaf Papers, Rogers' Notes) "about six feet high, broad- "shouldered, erect and well-proportioned, with dark-brown hair, a high "and open forehead, piercing dark-hazel eyes, and a large aquiline nose. "His step was measured and firm, and his whole bearing martial and "commanding. His character, which was formed in the field and camp, "remained unchanged through life. He was altogether a soldier, and "nothing but a soldier." The picture of this complete soldier and our earnest devoted clergyman participating in lotteries is not without interest for every generation.

[3] A false report. Washington outgeneralled the enemy, and Howe afterward retreated, but there was no general action.

12. Wrote home No. 6, by Mr. Plumb, to Mr. Foster & Mr. Hall—General Sinclair & Formay arrived in Camp about 9 o'Clock, rained in the Morning—purchased two Tickets No. 57,674 & 58,449 jointly with Col! Francis & Littlefield & Major Lithgow—sent my Journal[1] Home to this date.

13. Mr. Plumb set off for Boston at 4 ᵒClock P. M. Showry—two persons bro! in supposed to be Spies, who give an account that the Enemy are coming up 10,000 strong.—

14. The Regiment past muster—visited the Hospital at Mount Independence, the new Hospital about one third covered—250 long & 24 wide—warm and pleasant—

15. Sunday. Divine Service at Six ᵒClock, P. M. Matt. 16, 26.—pleasant—

16. Capt. Page &c arrived—receiv⁴ Letters by Him from Master Herrick to the 30ᵗʰ of May, fair & pleasant.

17. Wrote Home No. 7, & to Mr. Plumb by Post—visited Hospital A. M.—the Camp alarmed about noon by some firing without the Lines—two men were taken & some killed near MᶜIntoshes by some Indians, who were pursued by Scouts, who on their return met with Lieut Taylor who went out yesterday with a party of twelve men which was suddenly encompassed by them, exchanged several Shots wounded the Lieut: who escaped with two men, the others killed or taken—one dead Body found bro! in belonging to Col? Hale's Reg! —

18. This morning 8 of Lieut Taylors men came in, one swam over the Lake—another Col? Hale's men found in MᶜIntoshes field—General Schyler[2] came into

[1] It is unfortunate that the Journal was not preserved, even if the diaries had been lost. Many of the meagre entries indicate that important matter had been treated accordingly elsewhere.

[2] Philip Schuyler, of Albany, was a Major-General in the army. He commanded at Fort Edward when Ticonderoga was evacuated by St. Clair. He did not appreciate the quality of the New England troops, and excited the hostility of that section. He lacked the "soldier's eye"

Camp to-day—Major Lithgow[1] went to Fort George on Court Martial—Revd Allen of Pittsfield came into Camp.

19. One Harris of Col^o Hales Reg^t killed by an accidental discharge of his own Gun—this morning Capt Whitcomb came in who went out yesterday, bro^t an Indian Skalp killed by Taylors party—dined on roast Beef—fair Day—spent the evening in writing Letters by Capt Raymond—

20. Wrote Home N° 8 & to Rev. Forbes Mr. Herrick & Brother David—Major Hull dined with us upon Roast Beef &c—Capt Raymond set off for N. England; fair Day—

21. Appointed Chaplain[2] to gen^l Pattersons Brigade— fair Day—

22. Sunday.   Major Lithgow returned from Fort George, bro^t dispatches from Genl Washington to Schuyler, giving an account of the Enemies getting to Morrisania—confirming the late reports from Canada &c. fair Day but no Service, the men on fatigue & moving into Tents—
    GeneralSchuyler left Camp—

23. Dined at Genl Poors—receiv^d a letter from Revd Ward p^r Post—(Major Hull, Capt Gray & others dined with us—

24. Col^o Meads came into Camp about 12 ^oClock last

---

[1] William Lithgow, born in Georgetown, Maine, was a Major in the Continental line.   He was known as an ardent patriot.   After the war he was U. S. Attorney in Maine.

[2] Chaplain Smith (Guild's Life, p. 191) had a list of twenty-one Brigadier-Chaplains, dated Aug. 17, 1778.   Hitchcock's name was included.

---

and lost the confidence of his troops. Congress superseded him by Gates early in August. Gates was his personal enemy, and, though "sensible of the indignity," Schuyler showed great nobility of character and firm loyalty by doing everything to forward the work of his successor.

Night, informs that the Enemy were very near Crown-point at Sundown—The morning opens fair & very warm—warm all Day—

25. Col? Marshal dined with us—

26. Some men fired upon by Indians one killed & Skalped, one Skalped & came in wounded in several parts, a Shower P. M.

27. Rained last Night attended with much lightning—A Report of a number of Indians going to Skeene— very warm work upon our House—Shower at noon—

28. An account of two large Vessels sailing down the Lake—turned out at Gunfiring attended Prayers on the Brigade parade before Sunrise—warm Day— about Sunset one of their Vessels was discovered this side five mile point by a boat of ours & three a little below, upon seeing our Boat (80 Rods distant) they hoisted two, chased & fired upon it, several fires were exchanged which soon communicated to ye guard Boat who gave the Signal & an Alarm was fired—about half after 9 °Clock, I had just got into Bed, but immediately turned out & went parade, found the Brigade generally turned out & very Spirited—dismissed at half after eleven to lay on arms—Lieu! Huax deserted to the Enemy—

29. Sunday. Rise at gunfiring (½ past 2 °Clock) nothing happened[1] Attended prayers, dismissed at Sunrise, men all on Duty—

30. Alarmed at (blotted) °Clock last Night by firing from the Picket guard—it proved false—about 7 °Clock the guard Boats coming in—8 a number of Enemies Boats heave in sight, alarm Guns—Several Cannon discharged at the French lines at a party of Indians & others—Some Musketry with! the Picket drove

[1] One of those silly camp alarms, especially common among new troops and new organizations. Early in the Civil War General Burnside published a sensible and stringent order enjoining officers against the needless night-alarms which so often occurred.

in—at noon men dismissed to get Refreshment—
sent our Bagage to Mount Independ⁵—towards
Night two Ships, several Sloops a lare number of
Gun Boats & others stretch across the Lake within
one & ½ mile of the Jersey Battery—Mr. Shaw
came in with other Posts a little before Night,
receiv⁴ Letter from Home No. 3, Rev⁴ Foster & Fish
& Brother David—extreme Hot—

July 1. No disturbance last Night. Attended prayers before
Sunrise—the Enemy *in Statu quo*—good news from
Gen! Washington of the defeat of Hows Army, that
gen! Sullivan was in possession of Brunswick,
Gen! Green in possession of an advantage post
between that & Amboy—& that the Enemy were
fleeing precipitately —some firing at the mills—

2. The Mills & Block Houses evacuated as not tenable &
burnt—about 2 °Clock—
four Boats[1] came towards the Jarsey Battery—one
Cannon discharged at them, three Signal Guns from
the Enemies Ships—the Lines were soon maned
about three °Clock a firing between the Picket & a
party of Indians & Regulars it lasted more than half
an Hour the Picket retreated with the lost of about
five killed & Six wounded most of them bro⁵ in—the
Enemy followed up till Col? Francis Reg⁵ fired over
the Parapet some twice, some three Times—some
Cannon was discharged at them they soon retreated
—the men dismissed about Six °Clock—one Regular
Soldier was taken—two Hessians deserted came to
Mount Independ⁵ — they say the Enemy are 5600
strong.

3. A peacable Night, things *in Statu quo*—about 700
Maletia came into Camp P. Mr Hibbrt with them—

---

[1] According to Lieutenant Hadden (Rogers, p. 82) "The British
" Troops disembarked on the Tyconderoga side about Four Miles Short
" of it; and the Germans on the Mount Independence side." This was
two small corps of Germans retained with the British.

the Enemy[1] get possession of Mount Hope—Some Cannon fired at them opposite the Jersey Battery very warm—

4. The Enemy at work[2] on the rising ground fronting French Lines several Cannon fired at them— extreme hot—

5. Wrote Home by Mr. Shaw No. 9, the discovered on the Mount S. W. of Ti==some firing towards night— wind came in Cool & Crisp at 5 P. M. at N. W.— about 6 ºClock came for every man to furnish him-self with 24 rounds Extra & five Days provision, the Bumb drew in Shore & boats approach the Jersey Battery—at seven orders came for every man to be under Arms & march to their respective Alarm Posts—about nine orders for all to be ready with all their Effects to obey further orders[3]—with great Reluctance I left our new dwelling at past nine came over to Mount Independence, got the Baggage down to the wharf & put it on board the Schooner & Gundeloe

6. Sunday. at three ºClock hoisted Sail under a very small breeze with all our Vessels & set off for

[1] Frazer's Corps, under command of Major-General Phillips.

[2] July 4th. Hadden (p. 84) says the British made a road to the top of a high mountain called Sugar Loaf Hill. "This height commands both "*Mount Independence*, and *Tyconderoga* — The former at the distance "of 1600 yards, and the latter at 1400." To leave such a position not defended was a singular oversight on the part of our commanding officers. It was claimed that we had not men enough to fortify the place. It was a gross blunder, for, on the third, one of St. Clair's aids promised Washington "the total defeat of the enemy." Bancroft, Vol. V., 160. St. Clair himself had said, "Should the enemy attack us they "will go back faster than they came."

[3] Lieutenant Hadden (p. 84) agrees that it was on the night of the fifth that "the Rebels 3 or Thousand in number abandoned their Works at "Tyconderoga and Mount Independence leaving behind them all the "Guns, Stores, and Provisions, except 300 Barrels of Powder on board "one of their Vessels." Our chaplain gives a graphic sketch of his experience in the movement.

Skeene—the Land Army march at the same time for Castleton, Col? commands the rear Guard 500 men—arrived at Skeene two Clock P. M. in about an Hour the Enemies Gun boats came up & fired at one of our Row gallies, a brisk & mutual Canonade followed for near half an Hour during which time I was imployed amidst flying ball in getting some of my baggage on board a boat above the falls, which with difficulty I effected & put off up Wood Crick the shoalness of the Water & many loggs in it render it extremly difficult passing in boats ; set off between three & four °Clock & with much difficulty & hard labor, working all Night in the water we reached Fort Ann about

7. At ten °Clock, some boats in our rear cut off by Savages, the men mostly got in, but scattering partys continue to come in—about noon a Skirmish happened between a small Scouting party & a few Indians & some regulars we lost three, killed & four wounded,—some Stores came in from Fort Edward—fair Day—

8. Rested comfortably last Night, the Garrison was alarmed once but I did not turn out—about 9 °Clock a scouting party of a 100 men was sent out to go down the Crick to recover some lost Bagage, but soon met with a party of regular Troops about 300 a brisk firing came, 60 more went to reinfore them & then 30 & 20 more—the engagement last an Hour & half very warm—our loss was 10 killed and wounded —the Enemies supposed to be 40 or 50 killed and wounded, our men drove them from a little Breast≡ they had built up a hill—four of the Enemy were bro? in, viz D? Ciely of Lord Leigoniers Reg? well— Cap? Mongumery[1] wounded in the Knee & two privates dangerously wounded—a Council of war[2]

---

[1] William Stone Montgomery, Captain in the Ninth Foot British, was " an officer of great merit." He died in captivity.

[2] Chaplains did not generally attend at councils of war.

was called at which I was present, it was agreed upon
to evacuate to the Gurrison considering the weak
State it was in as to ammunition, & the large Reinforcement we had authentick assurance was on their
way to the Enemy—left Fort Ann in flames between
three & four °Clock P. M. travelled without Stoping
to Fort Edward 14 miles in a heavy rain reached it
at dark—

9. Lodged at Col? Snuths—General Fellows went for
    Fort Ann with a 1000 men—the fragment of our
    Army at this place in great Confusion without cover-
    ing—news of our main Body being at Castleton on
    Monday & of an Action there between Col? Warners
    Reg! & some Indians & Hessians—cloudy most of
    the Day—about Ten °Clock found quarters at Mr.
    Jaleds—bo! ½ a Lamb—

10. Lodged at Mr. Jilled's, attended Prayers with Cap!
    Farnum's men, Major Livingston came in from our
    Army brings account of an Action[1] between our rere
    guard & about 1400 Enemy, considerable loss both
    sides—also of Col? Francis fall in the field—an Ac-
    count of some Enemy at Fort Ann, but Gen! Fellows
    who went out yesterday with 600 men is about 4
    miles this side it—very warm—

11. Cap! Farnum was sent out a Scout with 40 men, on
    hearing some Enemy were betwixt this Fort George—
    a 100 loads were bro! fm thence yesterday as many
    gone for to Day—about 150 Malctia came in P. M.
    Accounts that the Enemy's main Body are at
    Skeene—rain⁴ from 5 °Clock till Night—

12. Rained all Night—Cap! Farnum returned, made no
    discovery—Gen! Nixon's[2] Brigade arrived (800) and

---

[1] The battle of Hubbardton occurred on the morning of the seventh.
It was a sharp contest. In all the wretched business of this retreat, there
was no greater loss than that we met in the death of Ebenezer Francis.
We cite Anburey's testimony: "whose death, though an enemy, will
"ever be regretted by those who can feel for the loss of a gallant and
"brave man."

[2] John Nixon, of Framingham, Mass., served at Louisburg in 1745.

encamped on the high land to the N. W. of the Fort[1]
the Gen[ls] from Ti= arrived, the Army left at Fort
Miller—some Maletia came from Berkshire County,
they are all on the move—

13. Sunday. Rained last Night—two prisoners bro[t] in
who say the Enemy have left Skeene & returned
to Ti=; that 15 officers were bro[t] dead, to Skeene;
no service; lowry Day

14. The parts of Regiments from Skeene ordered down to
Moses Crick five miles below Fort Edward—came
down about 5 ᵒClock P. M. Gen[!] Poor's Brigade came
up from Fort Miller—receiv[d] Letter from Mr. Plumb
—wrote Home No. 10.

15. Went down to Fort Miller to see our people found
them comfortable—dined at Gen[!] Pattersons, a per-

---

[1] At Fort Edward the American army rested; after a time, being
reorganized and reinforced, it regained confidence. Washington made
every sacrifice, freely risking his own campaign, to secure ultimate success for the Northern army. He sent in reinforcement Arnold, who was
then a gallant man, and Lincoln, who had the confidence of the Eastern
troops. Morgan's corps of picked riflemen was one important reinforcement. An excellent Brigade, under Glover, from the Continental line,
was taken from the central army, which could ill spare it. As has been
stated, the ill-fated Schuyler was replaced by Gates early in August.

But a chief factor in turning defeat into victory developed through the
incapacity of the enemy. Burgoyne's attack at Ticonderoga, his pursuit
to Hubbardton and Skenesborough was capable and energetic. This
was his last forcible or judicious conduct. Instead of moving around to
Lake George and following by the old roads and easy water communication, he halted a fortnight. "Britons never recede." Therefore he
must cut a direct road some twenty-eight miles through dense forests
and morasses to Fort Edward,—"Forty bridges" and one "log-work" of
two miles through morass indicate the toilsome work. He wore out his
victorious legions in these midsummer labors, while his defeated rival
was recovering strength.

He was at Lexington and Bunker Hill; at Stillwater he commanded the
First Brigade of the Massachusetts line.

son taken up for a Spy in Camp—two Waggons cut
off between ½ way & 5 mile Brook—Maletia come in
fast—fair Day—

16. Lodged on the floor at Mr. Day's—Rev.ᵈ Lyman came
into Camp—Fort George evacuated—

17. Wrote Home No. 11 & to Mr. Foster, our Brigade
came from Fort Miller up to the Island—

18. An Express from Col.º Warner that he has retreated
to Allington—wrote Home N.º 12 by Mr. Yancey
moved from Mr. Days down to Gen.ˡ Pattersons
opposite Chuylers alias Pattersons Island where the
Brigade is encamped—fair Day

19. Gen.ˡ Poor &c dined upon roast mutton & green peas—
warm—

20. Sunday. Divine Service¹ at ½ past 10 ºClock on
Patterson Island among the Trees, Neh: 4, 14 A M.
the Brigade generally attended ; two regulars & two
Tories bro.ᵗ in prisoners taken by some of our Indians
6 miles beyond Fort Ann—Gen.ˡ Poors servant &
Col.º Cilleys Son sent into Camp—Receiv.ᵈ a Letter
from Rev.ᵈ Cutler by the Post.

21. Letter from Lieu.ᵗ Chadburn gives account of the
Prisoners at Ti= Dodge, Raymond &c among
them—raind last Night, fair Day Col.º Putnams
Reg.ᵗ came in—

22. Wrote Home N.º 13, to Rev.ᵈ Cutler & Brothers ;
Gen.ˡ Fellows lodg.ᵈ here last Night is going Home
with part of the Maletia—

¹ Religious observances in campaigning often leave much to be desired.
When circumstances favor, the result accords happily. We may imagine
that this beaten army on this quiet Sabbath "among the trees" re-
sponded to the war-note, " Be not ye afraid of them," from the prophet
of Israel. The present writer recalls an equivalent experience in our
Civil War. The command had been engaged at Bull Run, losing heavily.
Ordered to Point of Rocks, Md., it commemorated its first quiet Sabbath, among the trees. A private soldier (since distinguished as a civil
engineer) preached, not after the manner of Israel's fiery prophet, but
with the fervor of a true Christian.

Gen! Arnold[1] came by & dined with us, fair Day

23. Twenty of our men taken about 7 miles this side Fort
Ann Yesterday moved into Gen! Patersons new
House on the Island, dined on an excellent Loin of
mutton.

24. Walked up to Gen! Nixon's Brigade—two men killed a
little above them towards Fort Edward by some
Indians—dined on pig—receiv[d] a Blanket of the
public Stores—receiv[d] of Mr. Conant 20[lb] two months
pay, paid Adjutant Francis 46 Dollars on the Col[s]
Account.

25. Wrote Home N[o] 14, by the Adjutant ; went down to
Fort Miller, dined with D[r] Hale, no occurrences—
fair Day

26. Six brass field pieces arrived in Camp—rained P. M—
we were alarmed about 2 °Clock by an attack at Fort
Edward—The Enemy, supposed near a 1000 crept
up & by Surprize fir[d] on the Picquet Guard, kill[d] &
Scalped them, the Guard retreated & were pursued
within 40 Rods of the Fort took away two women
from the House, killed, Scalped & mangled one in a
most inhumane man[r] ; four are missing ;

27. Sunday.   Divine Service at 11 °Clock, A. M. Is : 57,
21, at 5 P. M. Ps. 53, 1.   Some further accounts of
what hap ned at Fort Edward Yesterday—the Lieut :
who commanded the Piquet, Van Vechten, was killed,
scalped & cut his Hands off—& otherwise mangled—
The two Women, Mrs. Jenny M[c]Cray[2] & Widow
Cambell were going to meet the Enemy for protection, when they came up to them were shot &

---

[1] Benedict Arnold, of Norwich, Conn., Major-General in the army,
whose infamous treason is too well known.   Brave and erratic, rash and
destitute of moral principle, he was a comet among patriots.

[2] The murder of Miss Jane Maccrea was like many other Indian
atrocities, but it shocked the whole civilized world.   Burke used the
story with thrilling effect in the House of Commons, when he arraigned
the government for employing savages.

Scalp⁴ & most inhumanly boochered—the former found yesterday the other to Day—the advance Body of the   are on the flat about the Fort supposed about a 1000—

28. An Express from Fort Edward about break of Day, say they are Surrounded ; the account afterward proves groundless Wrote Home No. 15 per Post— Gen¹ Nixon's Larnerd's¹ & Tinbrook's² Brigade came down from Sneaks Creek, Learnard's encamp⁴ by Moses Creek—Nixon's on the rise N. E. of River—Brooks on S. W. Side. A Scout returned towards eveng—who went out yesterday, who give an account of a horrid murder of a Family about four N. E. of Fort Miller: the Father, Mother & six Children killed and left to be torn by the Hogs— Major Lithgow returned from Albany—

29. Col° Brewer with 150 men sent to Fort Miller to scout the woods N. E. Col° Cilley³ with the same number from Moses Creek to go east & meet them—about 9 °Clock a man & Boy killed & one wounded near Fort Miller by two lurking Fellows who contended about the Scalp of the Boy ; the man not Scalp⁴ ; 11 °Clock a small party y¹ went out back of Head q¹ˢ about ¾ of mile were fired upon by Indians one Corp¹ killed, private wounded—about the same time an Indian fired upon a Centry N. E. from Gen¹ Nixon

---

¹ Ebenezer Learned, of Framingham, Mass., was a captain in the French War. He led the third Massachusetts Regiment to Cambridge the day after the battle of Lexington. Congress commissioned him a Brigadier-General April 2, 1777. He was thanked with General Poor in Gates' order of September 26th for "the valiant behavior" of their brigades at Freeman's Farm.

² Abraham Ten Broeck, of Albany. He commanded a brigade at the battle of Bemis Heights.

³ Joseph Cilley, of Nottingham, N. H., afterward General, commanded the first N. H. Regiment. He was an active officer who distinguished himself at Bemis Heights, was at Stony Point, Monmouth, and in Sullivan's expedition against the Indians, serving through the war.

Brigade; wounded him in the Neck— a Small Scout
20 came in, which met with a party of Indian,s supposed 70, fired & killed one & ran—about 12 °Clock
alarmed by an Express from Fort Miller that they
were attacked by a number of Enemy but proved—
one of our Spies came in who says the Enemy had
almost cleared the road from Fort Ann which we
had blocked up—by one of our men who deserted
from the Enemy informs that they have 7500 encamped at Skeene who are to come forw^d as soon as
possible—our number now about 4000—

30. In Council of war held at six this morning it was
determined upon to retreat[1] to Surratoga—our Brigade was ordered to decamp immediately the huts to
rafted which was done, we left the Island at 12
°Clock, soon reached Fort Miller, one-half of the
Brigade tarried there, the other came down to M^r
Niels 3 miles I came with them & down to Genl
Schuylers—Genl Fornays[2] & Tinbrooks Brigade attacked in their rear by a party of the Enemy, one of
ours killed, one of Genl Arnolds Aid de Camps
wounded & two or three others—no great done—

---

[1] This was a good movement, bringing our army nearer to its natural
base and carrying the enemy farther from his.

[2] Fornay stands for Roche de Fermoi (or Fermoy), a Colonel from the
French army, made Brigadier-General by Congress. We have drawn
more blanks than prizes in our European officers, and Fermoi apparently was of the former sort. St. Clair's friends charged him with the
worst casualties in the retreat from Ticonderoga, in that he fired his
quarters at Mount Independence, thereby exposing the rear to Frazer's
pursuit. "One of the worst of the adventurers was this very General
Fermoy, who brought disaster upon the rear of St. Clair's army after the
successful retreat from Ticonderoga." Smith's St. Clair, I., 65 n.
Gates dismissed Fermoi with a letter to Hancock September 14, 1777,
containing this shrewd diplomatic praise: "I have much respect for the
"Long Service and Rank of General Fermoi and wish circumstances
"had made it convenient to have retained him here." (Gates' MS. Papers,
N. Y. Historical Society. Rogers' MS. Notes.)

Gen! Lincoln[1] came up—met with Mr Shaw at the Barracks, Letter from Home & Rev⁴ Morrel & Brother David—

31. Lodged at Gen! Schuylers[2] went up to Mr. Niels the Army pass⁴ down the other side, except Gen! Poors Brigade which stopt here—Gen! Glovers Brigade[3] arrived at Surratoga—

August 1. Lodged at Mr. Niels last night; the Brigade came down & encamp⁴ by the Barracks, 2 Miles, Gen! Glover & Col? Wigglesworth[4] came in—heard of D⁴ Leonards suicide, one man wounded & partly Scalped the east side of the River—rained a little

2. Lodged last Night with D⁴ Wingate—Mrs. Ranken cut Her throat—Capt Whitcombe came in after a weeks scout with four men, observed the Enemy's movements from Skeene, they arriv⁴ at Fort Edward to Day—fair Day—

3. Sunday. Wrote Home N? 16, by Mr. Shaw—we were alarmed about 7 °Clock by some firing towards M⁴ Niels. Major Hull commanded an advance party there they were surprized by some Indians as they were coming off, Gen! Paterson with His Brigade & part of Glovers were to support them, in mean Time

---

[1] Benjamin Lincoln, of Hingham, Mass., was a Major-General in the army, and after September 29th was second in command under Gates. He had fair military ability and great force of character.

[2] Schuyler's house was afterwards the scene of Burgoyne's last orgy, in company with his mistress and military friends. In the morning he ordered it fired with the barn; for which he has been much censured. Other critics, not partial to him, claim that the burning was a military necessity. See Kingsford History of Canada, VI., 262-3. The story of the supper, commonly received, is disputed in Baxter's note to *Digby's Journal*, p. 43.

[3] Of the Continental line.

[4] Edward Wigglesworth, of Ipswich, Mass., was commissioned Colonel of Thirteenth Massachusetts Regiment November 6, 1776. He resigned March 10, 1779.

a party of 40 was sent out about 2 Miles S. W. were attacked by some Tories, some were killed, some wounded—Major Hulls party lost three, some wounded—the Brigade return'd from M: Niels P. M. the Army set from Surratoga between 4 & 5 °Clock, we marched thro' the mud & some rain till 12 °Clock when we arrived at Still Water, encamped on the wet ground—

4. Mr. Shaw set off this morning—an alarm at 9 °Clock occasioned by some Inhabitants moving in—two Tories bro'. in taken about 6 miles East, with passes & Certificates, in Arms—fair Day—

5. Rained most of the Day—by a prisoner who deserted from Ti= we learned that one of our people had found a pocket Book, belonging to a British Officer in which was found a return of all they had lost in the several Skirmishes since our Retreat—viz—at Houghberton 292 killed & died of their wounds— at Fort Ann 96, many officers among them; also that they could find only 19 dead among our Slain— four Tories bro'. in bound one of which is a Clergyman—

6. Visited the Hospital—considerable rain—began to break ground on the flat—no remarkable occurrences

7. Drew from the Store one pair Shoes two of Stockings &c receiv'd a Letter from Rev'd Ward dated July 23ʳᵈ very warm Col° Long[1] & Reg'. left Camp—

8. Alarmed this morning by a Major with two Boy & a Waggon being taken east side of the River bound to Cambridge—from deserters from the Enemy—a Sergeant & three privates, Hanoverians left Fort

---

[1] Pierse Long, of Portsmouth, N. H., of Irish stock, whence so much of our fighting blood has come, Colonel first N. H. Regiment. He repulsed the ninth British in the action of July 7th (see Stone's Burgoyne, p. 26), under Lieutenant-Colonel Hill. On the surrender at Saratoga, Hill stole the colors of his regiment, secreted them in his baggage, and carried them home. For this service he was appointed aid to the king. See Rogers' note, Hadden, p. 90.

Edward last Monday—inform that the Enemy have 6500 there, that they are preparing to come on but much embarassed for want of Carriages—P. M. a young man & his Father coming to Camp on the east side the   was shot & Scalp^d —Capt Warren who went out in the Morning with a Company Infantry, fell in with about 12 Indians He having advanced with only 4 men, briskly, engaged them held his Ground, lost one & killed an Indian & bro^t in his Scalp—

9. Capt Warren receiv^d the public thanks of the Genl for his spirited behavior yesterday Excessive hot ; news of an Engage^t near Fort Schuyler—

10. Sunday.   No Service, not well to Day—warm—

11. Wrote Home N° 17 & to Revd Ward per Post—very warm—

12. Genl St Clair set of, for Philadelphia—Genl Larnard & his Brigade marched for Fort Schuyler—Genl Lincoln came to Camp—very warm a Shower

13. Genl Arnold set out for Fort Schuyler—very warm

14. Showry very warm, no remarkable occurrence, to Day Col^o Brewer went out to Scatter rock after Cattle

15. Rained last Night, agreeable to Genl Orders the Army turned out at 2 °Clock, threw their Boards together in heaps—about Six set Still Water¹, marched to half Moon where we arrived about 4 °Clock P. M. rained most of the Day—Gen^{ls} Glover Nixon & Poors Brigades stoped at the Landing 6 Miles below Still Water, our Brigade came past two Branches on to Van Schoiks Island—

16. Lodged at Mr. Van Shoicks an Elegant House on an Island of best Land formed by the 2nd & 3rd Branch of the Mowhawk River—this morning a despatch ar-

---

¹ This was the last backward movement of our army. After Gates took command he returned to Stillwater. At Stillwater we rested, and when the enemy finally advanced to Freeman's Farm, he received his fatal repulse. Bancroft, V., 181, puts the place nine miles above Albany.

rived from Bennington[1] informs that Gen! Frazer with his flying Camp was within 5 miles of the Meeting House; that we were almost round them— Mr. Plumb came into Camp P. M. by whom I receiv'd Letters from Home & Rev'd Willard—

17. Sunday. No Service to Day, the men all employed, receiv'd Letter from Phebe Parsons, Gen! Lincoln— marched to the Grants—

18. Wrote Home N? 18, by Mr. Davis of C$^{ap}_{arm}$ to Rev'd Willard, Cousin Phebe & Brother Moses—An Express from Bennington inform that they had an Engagement that we had taken 400 prisoners & four Field pieces—

19. By Express this morning have following list of Prisoners taken at Bennington, viz—1 Lieu! Col? —1 Major 8 Cap^{ts}—14 Lieut? 4 Ensigns—2 Cornets—1 Judge Advocate—1 Baron—2 Canadian officers—6 Surgeons—37 British Soldiers—398 Hessians—38 Canadians—151 Tories—4 Brass Field pieces—80 killed— 200 wounded & fell into our Hands—   Gen! Gates[2]

[1] Burgoyne's expedition under Colonel Baum to Bennington was badly planned, and worse executed. Lieutenant Hadden aptly says (*Journal*, p. 136) that it was unjust to lay the whole fault on Breymann — who was much blamed for his tardy march in support —"when almost every per-"son concerned seems to have had a principal share in the disaster." It was the beginning of the end of the British. They not only lost guns and prisoners, but the more essential loss of opportunity to buy from the country horses and wagons, which were badly needed.

The action had many elements of romance. Stark disobeyed orders, or he would not have been there, to cut off Baum. His apothegm dooming Molly Stark to widowhood was worth a song of Homer to the States. In his report, he said. "we have returned a proper compliment in the "above action for the Hubbartown engagement." It was one of the few successes of militia against regular troops.

[2] Horatio Gates was a Major-General born in England and a godson of Horace Walpole. He was regularly trained in the British army, taking part in Braddock's expedition. He is entitled to credit for good generalship in securing the surrender of Burgoyne, as will appear. He commanded also in the worst defeat of the whole war, which occurred at Camden. His intrigues against Washington, seeking the chief command

arrived into Camp this Evening—visited the Hospital—new City—fair & pleasant Genl̤ Nixon's & Glovers Brigades came on to the first Island—

20. Genl̤ Schuyler let Camp, bound to the southward—went to see the great falls said to near a hundred feet perpendicular—catch out in a heavy shower—

21. Col̤ Brewer, who was sent with the women to guard Stores to Bennington, returned with 40 Tories taken in the Action there—Returned to Mess with Col̤ Littlefield extreme hot

22. Very hot to Day—visited Hospital at new City—

23. Two Tories bro̤ in

24. Sunday. Divine Service at 5 °Clock P. M. 1 Cor: 15, 19. Receiv̤ a Letter from Mr. Foster per Post—Wrote Home N̤ 19 & to Mr. Foster by Post—4 Hessian deserters[1] bro̤ & 4 Waldeck prisoners taken

---

[1] Desertion troubled Burgoyne as his order shows August 21, 1777 :
" The general zeal of this Army in the cause of the King and the " British constitution, is too apparent to admit a suspicion of the crime ' of Desertion, ever entering into the men's minds, except when they are " intoxicated, or imposed upon by Emissaries of the Enemy . . such " Emissaries have dared to intrude in the Camp, by spurious promises ". . perhaps by a readiness in the German language. . . In regard " to Deserters themselves, all outposts, Scouts and working Parties, of " Provincials and Indians, are hereby promised a reward of twenty " Dollars for every Deserter they bring in ; and in case any Deserter " should be killed in the pursuit, their scalps are to be brought off."— Orderly Book, p. 79. September 30 (p. 123), Burgoyne pays his respects to the drivers : " They are also to be informed that the first Deserter " taken belonging to them will be hanged up immediately."

---

for himself, aroused the just indignation of the whole country. We may consider that he possessed fair military ability, though our diarist (p. 109, MS.) participates in the prejudice against him current at the time. Kingsford (History Canada, VI., 229), who may be accounted disinterested, says, " although there is nothing to warrant the mention of Gates' name with very high laudation, at the same time there is no just reason " for the exaggerated depreciation of his character, which is constantly " to be met in United States biographies." He assumed command, displacing Schuyler at the time stated by Hitchcock.

near Surratoga by a Sergeant & 4 men—Several
Tories—Receiv^d a Letter this Evening from Capt
Batchelder wrote to Him by the Post—

25. Went to Albany in the P. M. rained most of the P. M.
put up with Mr Plumb at Mr Roorbeck's news that
the Enemy left Fort Stanwix left their Tents Stand-
ing & all heavy Bagage—

26. Dined at Dr Potts's—returned to Camp P. M. rainy
most of the Day—

27. Report y^t our Troops have possession of Long Island
&c—

28. Dined at Genl Gates's[1] — Eighty Connecticut light
Horse came into Camp, were ordered over to Pitts-
town half way to Bennington—visited Hospital—

29. No noticeable occurrence to Day

30. Eight Hundred Riflemen[2] arrived to Genl Poors
Camp—Mr. Shaw & Pearson came into Camp this
Evening receiv^d Letters f^m Home of ye 8, 11, & to
ye 25th; from Revd Morrell to 22 Aug^t :

31. Sunday.   Divine Service at 11 °Clock A. M. Jer:
2, 19, at 4 P. M. Exod : 15, 3, very Warm.
Do thou, great Liberty, inspire our Souls
& make our Lives in thy possession happy
or our Deaths glorious in thy just Defence

September 1.   A Troop of Connecticut Horse came into
Camp—Genl Lincoln & Parmer came from Benington—visited Hospital attended funeral of a Sergeant
of Col^o Bradfords Reg^t just at Night a Flagg came
in from Burgoine on the subject of Torys being
killed in cool blood.

---

[1] Our author evidently was *persona grata* in all the relations of life.
He had the true social gift and was received accordingly everywhere, as
may be seen in these scant records.   Chaplains are either greater or less
than the place demands.   If they are superior men, they become excellent military ministers, or the reverse follows.

[2] This must have been Morgan's command, though the number is
probably overstated.

2. Prisoners bro! in from the Germane flats taken as Spies—Accounts of Gen! Washington passing Philadelphia—Receiv? Letter from Rev? Ward & Brother David, & wrote to them by Mr Shaw—Wrote Home N? 20, sent a 20 Doll Bill—wrote to Rev? Morrill & Mrs. Francis—

3. Dined at Gen! Glovers with Brigadier Palmer & D? Taylor wrote to Cap! Batchelder—

4. Accounts receiv? y! ye Enemy are bumbarding Baltimore—Brigade mustered & viewed at Night by Brigadier Palmer & D? Taylor—

5. Went to Gen! Poors Brigade, Dined at Col? Brooks's —one of Cap! Maybury's men ran from the Enemy say they are coming down.

6. Receiv? Letter from M? Foster p? Post—

Gen! Orders Sept 6, 1777

The Gen!s commanding Divisions, & the Gen!s & Col?s commanding Brigades to see y? ye commanding Officers of Regiments & Corps have every thing in immediate readiness for a March y? w? Gen! Orders[2] are issu? , ye Army may have only to Strike t! Tents, load their Baggage & instantly on ye word being given, march off ye Ground—

A very large Army of Maletia[3], with a Brigade of Continent Troops, under ye Command of Gen! Lin-

---

[1] John Brooks, M. D., LL. D., of Medford, Mass., was a brilliant soldier and an accomplished man. A fellow-student of Count Rumford,— the bent of his mind and his education made him the associate of Steuben, when the latter became the Inspector-General of the army in 1778. They formed the system of tactics. In this campaign, he was Colonel of the Seventh Massachusetts Regiment.

[2] The abounding rhetoric of the order does not exaggerate the rising of the militia to repel Burgoyne's invasion. Through the Connecticut valley and eastward to Middlesex and Essex in Massachusetts, the hardy freemen mustered at the call of Washington. They assisted our campaign by their reinforcement in the battles, and yet more by their operations on the communications of the British. The enemy's supplies were practically cut off before the surrender at Saratoga.

[3] Whatever the middle and southern colonies may have thought of the

coln & Gen! Starks, being now assembled on y^e
Grants, & every necessary preparation for t^r acting
in Concert with this Army, upon ye point of being
compleated, the whole force must be prepared to
march upon ye Shortest notice—

To drive ye Enemy with Disgrace & defeat back to
Canada, is ye Object of the present Campaign—What
has been so Successfully begun under Gen! Starks &
Col^o Warner to ye Eastward, & by Gen! Harkemer &
Col^o Gansivoort to ye Westward cannot with ye Bless-
ing of Hvn, fail to be equally prosperous in y^e
Hands of ye Gen^{ls} & Soldiery appointed to face y^e
Enemy's main Army to ye North—

If the murder of aged Parents with their Innocent
Children—If mangling the Blooming Virgin &
Inoffensive youth be Incitments to Revenge!
If the Righ^{ts} Cause of Freedom, & ye Happiness of
Posterity, be motives to Stimulate The Army to con-
quer their Mercenary & merciless Foes—! The Time
is now come when they are called upon by t^r Country,
by their Gen^{ls}, by every Reason humane & Divine,
to vanquish their Enemies—

Each State in particular & ye grand Convention of the
united States in general are at this moment Indis-
criminally employed to provide their Armies with
every Comfort & necessary that can possibly be
procured—

Duty, Gratitude & Honor must Ergo inspire the Heart
of every Officer and Soldier, to do Justice to ~~this~~ their
much injured Country!

---

militia of New England, the testimony of one of our chief antagonists
was clear and decisive. Sir William Howe (Narrative p. 18) says,
" Besides, the provinces of New England are not only the most populous,
" but their militia, when brought to action, the most persevering of any
" in all North America; and it is not to be doubted that General Wash-
" ington, with his main army, would have followed me into a country
" where the strength of the Continent, encouraged by his presence, would
" have been most speedily collected."

7. Sunday. Shower last Night with much Lightning—
Divine Service at 11 ⁰Clock A. M. at 4 P. M. Exds:
5, 16 Ezra 9, 13, 14—Orders came out at Eight
Clock in Evening for all Tents to be Struck & the
Army to be under way at Gunfiring—Wrote Home
pʳ Post Nᵒ 21 & to Mʳ Foster—

8. Rose at 4 ⁰Clock, Tents Struck & load at Gunfiring—
marchᵈ off the Island at Nine, forded the Sprorts, to
half Moon where we joined Genˡˢ Govers & Nixon's
Brigade, go on to the Widow peoples's; about 4
Miles—where Genˡ Arnolds Division & Colᵒ Morgans
Riflemen joined, halted half Hour—go about four
Miles further & encamp—a fine Day & the men in
very high Spirits—three Tories escaped from the
main Guard last Night.

9. Rose at 4 Tents & Baggage loaded, the Army marched
off at eight ⁰Clock—reached Still Water at 11.
Colᵒ Francis Regiment ordered on the Hill on the
east side the River—cool Day—Colᵒ Baldwin[1] began
a bridge a Cross the River in yᵉ afternoon—

10. A very rainy Night, my Tent blew over—Colᵒ Beadle
from the Grants mentions that 45 Families of St
Francis Indians had movᵈ to Coos to avoid fighting
agᵗ us—The Bridge finished by the middle of the
Afternoon—

11. Genˡ Starks's Brigade under command of Colᵒ Ashley
(600) arrived, took possession of the hight Colᵒ Francis Regᵗ order to join the Brigade—came over just at
Night,—The whole Army ordered to be under Arms
at retreat beating

12. The Army decamped from Still Water at Six &
marched up the road two & out about half a Mile to
the westward of the road, behind Becmuses[2], en-

---

[1] Jeduthan Baldwin, of Woburn, Mass., was a Colonel of Engineers in
the Continental corps. His command is spoken of as a "regiment of
artificers."

[2] This strong position at Behmus' Heights was intrenched and became
the citadel of our army. Stone puts the distance three miles north of

camped of the heights— Goodale returned & bro! me a Letter from Home dated Sep! 2ⁿᵈ—rainy—the Bridge bro! up—

13.   Invitation to dine at Headquarters while I was there 2 Prisoners were bro! in from near Surratoga from whence four were bro! in the morning—by their accounts the Enemy are moving tow⁴ us, their army all collected near Surratoga—various in their Accounts of their Strength—I saw a Letter to the Gen! from one M! Clerk of N. Perth, the Grants, a Clergyman who is gone out with protection to offer to Tories who will return—who says the road from Fort Edward is lined with Tents eno' to hold 16000 men—That Gen! Lincoln is possessed of Fort Ann, Skeene & some say Fort George" This is report

Col? Hale is under confinement at Albany—entrenchments throwing up, from yᵉ Hill to yᵉ River—

Sunday 14.   Divine Service at 4 °Clock P. M. l's: 115, 11 fair Day—Wrote Home N? 22 pr Post.—

15.   Two Tories bro! in to Day—The British Troops at Surratoga, Hessians opposite to M! Niel's—Drew a pair of Breeches from the Store at 6 Dolls & a ⅓— Col? Colman who went out Saturday with 300 men to observe the Enemy's motions, returned & says they have 1000 Tents, that they struck them all except a few & moved at 12 °Clock & their rear started off at two, marched this way—in conseq⁵ of this Intelligence the ordered that the whole Army to lay upon their Arms, & to turn out at 4 °Clock tomorrow morning, expecting an Attack about that Time, The Army are in fine Spirits—dined at Headquarters—

Stillwater.   The action of September 19th was at Freeman's Farm, further north.   The action of October 7th, and the last, was in the final attempt of Burgoyne to turn this position.

(Diary of Enos Hitchcock, D. D., to be continued.)

(Diary of Enos Hitchcock, D. D., continued from page 134.)

16. The Army turned out agreeable to orders & went to
their Alarm Posts but not Enemy appear—a Deserter
or Prisoner bro! in last night—the Enemy within Six
Miles of us—Gen! Starks came into Camp last Even-
ing, informs that Gen! Lincoln is gone to Ti= that
Col? Brown [1] with a 1000 men is gone to Fort
George = Orders for two days provisions to be
cooked = this Afternoon Flagg came in to bring
Cap! Watkins & Lain on Parole for two months—one
British Soldier & two Tories taken & bro! in—one
Tory Ensign—Wrote Home N? **22.** by Mr. Appleby.

17. The morning a quarrel hapned between one Sam! Hem-
menway & Dudley Broadstreet of Cap! Thorn's
Company, the former thrust a Knife into the Neck of
the latter, cut the jugelar vein partly, a dangerous
wound! This Evening orders for the whole Army to
have their Tents & baggage loaded at 4 the morning
& be under Arms—

18. Turned out & loaded Baggage &c at 4, [2] a fine Morning—about Sunrise Gen! Arnold's Division marched
past in the Road by River & part in western Road
the Carpenters go forward to build Bridges—our
Brigade repaired at 7 °Clock to their Alarm Post—
the advance Body of the Enemy said to be within

---

[1] John Brown of Sandisfield, Mass., a vigorous patriot, under the orders
of Gen. Lincoln, surprised the outposts of Ticonderoga, set free 100
American prisoners, captured four companies of regulars with stores and
cannon. He destroyed a number of boats and an armed sloop; altogether he struck a hard blow at the British. Brown foresaw the treachery
of Arnold, and left the Northern army on account of his detestation of
the future traitor.

[2] This daily practice of breaking camp added much to the mobility of
Gates' command. He could not know just where or when the enemy
would appear and was always ready. It deceived the enemy. After
Freeman's Farm, because the Americans packed baggage, Burgoyne
thought they were about to run.

two [3] Miles the main about *three* [4] — Cap.! Chadwick
came across 33 of the Enemy getting Potatoes,[1] fired
& killed one, wounded 3 & took 8—Gen.! Arnold with
Division went near their Camp but nothing capital
happened—fine Day.

19.   This Day about ten °Clock accounts receiv.ᵈ that the
Enemy are advancing [2] — the Army all under Arms
—a large body Col? Morgan's men & others, sent
out—a Skirmish began between them & a Body of
Enemy at half after one, lasted half an Hour, very
hot about 17 minutes, beat the Enemy of the ground
—took some well & all the wounded—at 40 minutes
after three & lasted three Hours very hot—we drove
them half a mile—constant reinforcements on both

---

[1] This potato skirmish was exaggerated by the British.   Anburey puts
the killed and wounded near thirty (Digby's Journal and citation from
A. p. 270).   Anburey apparently forgets that soldiers within three miles
of an active enemy are liable to be hurt, whether digging potatoes or
levelling their muskets.

[2] The battle of Freeman's Farm, often called the first battle of Stillwater, or of Saratoga, was the turning point in Burgoyne's career, and it
virtually decided the fate of his army.   Like most European tacticians,
when moving in America, he does not appear to have availed of his
Indians, scouts, or other means, to find out where his enemy was located,
or how posted.   On the nineteenth of September he made "a scout," as
he called it, "if occasion served, to attack the rebels on the spot."   There
was an elaborate formation in three columns about half a mile apart (see
Lamb's Journal of the American War, p. 158); the right consisting of
light troops from the various regiments with Breyman's German riflemen,
commanded by Gen. Fraser; the centre comprising 20th, 21st, 62d regiments, commanded by Gen. Hamilton and led by Burgoyne in person;
the left bringing the British artillery with the remaining Germans, and
commanded by Generals Phillips and Riedesel.
According to Digby's Journal, p. 270, the British had intelligence at
daybreak that Morgan was posted three miles from them, with the main
body a half mile in his rear, very strongly posted.   By all American accounts, Morgan was sent out after the British advance begun.   Hitchcock's statement is strictly correct, so far as it goes.   One hundred
"Picquets" under Major Forbes 9th British (see Hadden, p. 162) were
severely punished by Morgan, at one or half-past one, who in turn was

sides made Success various, we took three field pieces
from them but not be able to bring them off being no
road, they retook them—the action ceased, as night
approached—tis impossible to determine what Success as we can; find either their or our loss, it must
be considerable on both—many wounded of both
brot in—among the Slain Col; Colburn & Adams—

20. This morning agreeable to orders, all turned out at
three °Clock. Struck Tents & loaded all baggage
ready to move at 4—the Brigade repair to their
Alarm Post at break off Day & their tarried all Day
—the Baggage sent down to Still Water — the
wounded to Albany, about 160 of ours between
twenty & thirty of theirs were brot off the field yesterday—the dead said to be 40—a hundred Indians
came from Albany—fair Day—two or three Deserters
came in say that Gen; Burgoyne is wounded in the
Body—

Sunday 21. Turned out & went to alarm post at four
°Clock this morning, Brigade remained there most of
the Day, several small Showers—news of Col° Brown
taking the French lines &c—thirteen Cannon [1] dis-

---

[1] Digby (p. 276) says "they fired 13 heavy guns, which we imagined
"might be signals for an attack; and which would be the most fortunate
event that we could have wished, our position being so very advanta-
"geous." The "National Salute," which disturbed the British then,
has been heard many times since.

---

repulsed by a battalion wheeled over from Fraser on the British right.
Morgan's riflemen pressed on through the woods and struck the left of
the British centre. Gates, from his headquarters, had sent forward three
New Hampshire battalions. It is stated that as many as nine regiments
were directed by Arnold. At 3.40 P. M. the battle became general and
raged for three hours or more. The contest was severe for the possession of the clearing known as Freeman's Farm. The Americans had no
artillery and seized the British guns several times. They could not bring
them off, nor turn them in their own favor, having no lintstocks. Burgoyne's centre was hammered hard, the 62d regiment being nearly anni-

charged on the Occasion & three Cheers given—the
Indians bro! in two Tories painted like themselves—
who were upon Centry with the Enemy, Gen! Gates
delivered them up to their handling, they drove them
shouting & whooping thro the Street—the number of
killed & wounded three hundred eighteen in the late
Action— Received Letters from Capt Batchelder
& Cousin Phebe pr Post—

22. Turned out at three this morning Struck Tents &
loaded Baggage—about noon pitched them again—
Indians bro! in two regular Prisoners & one Scalp—
paraded thro the road with them—Wrote Home pr
Post No 23 not numbred—To Capt Batchelder Red
Fish & the Printer—rained P. M.

23. Alarmed by discharge of severl Cannon in the
Enemy's Camp—dined at Headquarters — Indians
bro! in Seven Tories—

---

hilated. Morgan's riflemen, posted in trees, made sad havoc among the
opposing officers. Generally the British could not use their favorite
weapon, the bayonet. When the centre was about exhausted, Reidesel,
moving to the sound of the guns from the left, poured a heavy fire into
the right flank of the Americans attacking the centre. The attacking
troops staggered, and the British drove them from the field by a well-
directed charge of bayonets. Fraser and Breyman wished to pursue and
follow up the advantage, but were recalled by Burgoyne's positive order.
He was much censured by both parties for this act. It was nearly dark,
and the movement could not have made much difference to the campaign, but it would have changed the aspect of this engagement somewhat. Burgoyne claimed the victory, which all authorities have since
denied him. The British loss was estimated at 500 to 600, and the
American at about 320. The results were greater than could be comprehended in any single action. The morale of both armies was changed.
There was no lack of courage on either side, but Burgoyne's force included the flower of European troops. Stedman (American War, I., 323)
fairly states his opponent's case. " No solid advantages resulted to the
" British troops from this encounter. The conduct of the enemy con-
" vinced everyone that they were able to sustain an attack in open plains
" with the intrepidity, the spirit, and the coolness of veterans. For four
" hours they maintained a contest hand to hand."

24. Orders to strike Tents & load Baggage at Ten ᵒClock this morning occasioned by Deserters, who say the Enemy are coming on—Indians broᵗ in three Tories —nothing of Consequence happened—Good news from the Southard that Howe had lost 3000 in the late Action we 1000 &c—Genᵗ. Lincoln's Troops came in—Maletia from Berkshire Count came up—Army in high Spirits—

25. Indians broᵗ in two Tories—rained most of the P. M—

26.¹ The Indians broᵗ in eleven Prisoners, Hessians & Tories, two of our own men & two Scalps—Maletia come in fast—

27. One Deserter & one of our men from the Enemy— Cool—

Sunday 28. This morning at ten ᵒClock the Camp was alarmed by the discharge of a Cannon in the Enemy's Camp—men at their Alarm Posts all Day—Dr. Jones & Mr. Shaw ; receivᵈ Letter from Home, Mr. Herrick

---

¹ Gates was a fair soldier, but one of the meanest of men. On the 26th he issued his congratulatory order . . . " the General has not been " properly at leisure to return his grateful thanks to Gen: Poor's & Gen. " Learned's Brigades, to the regiment of riflemen and to Colᵒ Marshall's " regiment for their valiant behaviour in the action of the 19th inst." (Digby's Journal, p. 283.) No mention of Morgan, who had borne the brunt of the fray, nor of Arnold, who was heroic under fire, though his generalship was criticised. Gates had studied for a week how to mortify these men, whom he hated.

Anburey's statement (Travels in America, I., 418) is interesting. " The " courage snd obstinacy with which the Americans fought, were the as- " tonishment of every one, and we now become fully convinced, they are " not that contemptible enemy we had hitherto imagined them, incapable " of standing a regular engagement, and that they would only fight be- " hind strong and powerful works."

It was proven that the superior training, discipline and organization of the British army could be fairly met and sometimes overcome by the better intelligence, marksmanship and adaptability of the Americans.

& Mrs. Francis by them with my Horse—from Mr.
Foster & Brother David by Post, wrote to them by
Him—

29. This morning two Hessian Sergeants one Drumers &
a private—Six Hessians made Prisoners & a number
of Horses—fair Day—

30. This Day Six Canadians made Prisoners & one Regular
—William Dodge retaken—several Horses bro! in—
dined at Col? Brooks's

October 1.   two Hessian Deserters this morning—Rev! Mr.
Jones, Col? Stone &c dined with me—fair Day—

2. This morning two Hessian Deserters came in—Set off
for Albany about Ten, dined at the new City got into
town Sunset—warm Day—

3. Receiv! of the Paymaster Gen! 312 Dollars & half—drew
from the Continental Store 5 yds of Black Broad
Cloth at 7 & ¼ Dollars p! y!, 3 D? Serget at one
D? 2 Sticks Mohair 2?, 2 oz: thread 2?—Wrote
Home N? 24. to Mr. Herrick & Mrs Francis by Mr.
Shaw, sent Home 200 Dollars—fifty Prisoners bro! in
to town taken near Surratoga among whom was one
Cap!, two Lieut?, one Ensign—

4. Returned to Camp : dined at new City—two Deserters
came in.

Sunday October 5.   Divine Service at 4 °Clock P. M.
Matt 5. 32   this Day Six Hessian Deserters came in
& four of our men made their escape—

6. Wrote Home N? 25 pr Post to Mr Foster & Brother
Moses—this P. M. a Skirmish between Scouting par-
ties a reinforcement went out from Gen! Glovers [1]
Brigade drove the Enemy into their Lines killed three

---

[1] Brigadier General John Glover of Salem, Mass., was little, but strong,
a good soldier and general. One of the best organizers and disciplina-
rians in the Continental line. Washington sent him with his brigade to
the Northern army, when in its direst needs, after the retreat from
Ticonderoga.

or four,[1] we had four wounded—the remainder of
Gen! Lincolns party came to Camp—fair Day—eight
Deserters four of our own men—

7. This afternoon about two oClock, the Camp alarmed,
repair to their Alarm Posts—the Enemy advanced on
our left [2] — Col? Scammels & Hales Reg⁵ were sent
out to observe their Motions & attack them, a Scattering fire began a little before four oClock, at half
after four it came on very heavy & lasted till Dark—
our Troops drove them ¾ of a Mile, pursued to their
Encampment & took possession of one of the Hessian
Camp with all its Tents, Baggage

8. Little happened today, but loose firing—thirty Deserters came in—I went over the Ground where the
Battle was, found a number of the dead Stript—

----

[1] This skirmish is reported by Digby (p. 286): " I went out on a large
"forage for the army, and took some hay near their camp. On our re-
"turn we heard a heavy fire and made all the haste possible with the
"forage. It was occasioned by some of our rangers falling in with
"theirs; our loss was trifling."

[2] History labors long in getting itself recorded. The battle of Behmus'
Heights is a misnomer. The Heights were fully one mile and a quarter
south of the actual battle-ground (Stone, Burgoyne's campaign, p. 71) and
were the headquarters of Gates. The second battle of Stillwater, which
will be known always as Behmus' Heights, was begun 225 rods southwest
of Freeman's Farm and ended on the site of the first action. The
British had thrown up half-moon redoubts to secure the Freeman clearing, their citadel and centre. A straggling entrenchment ran eastward
almost to the Hudson, where the most of the artillery was strongly
posted. It was a strong position and Gates was shrewd enough not to
attack it.
Burgoyne had to do something, and after serious councils he determined to make a strong reconnaissance and turn the American left, if
possible. Riedesel and Fraser had advised — Phillips withholding
opinion — an immediate retreat. Burgoyne was to decide the main ques-
tion after trying the fighting. He could muster only 1500 men and pro-
tect his camp properly. He took 700 of Fraser's, 300 of Breyman's, and
500 of Riedesel's, with eight guns and two howitzers. The advance was in
three columns; Fraser commanded the right, which was swinging around

Gen! Lincoln badly wounded in the Leg—both bones
bro! to pieces—eight field pieces & two ammunition
Wagons were bro! in last Night—

      the number of our killed

wounded   their killed

wounded   Prisoners

See Octr 13.

9. This morning about forty Deserters came in who
inform that the Enemy left their Encampment between twelve °Clock & Day—we soon took possession of it—& found a number of Hospital Tents & a
large Barn with 340 wounded,[1] Doct<u>rs</u> & Nurses &c
—some provisions, Arms &c—our Carpenters went
forward to repair Bridges, began to rain about Ten
°Clock last till Evening—Wrote Home N°. 26 by M<u>r</u>
Cleaveland—

---

[1] Facsimile of Burgoyne's letter surrendering this hospital may be seen
Nar. and Crit. America, VI., 310.

---

to get the advantage of Gates. Phillips and Riedesel were in the centre,
but Burgoyne led here in person. Wilkinson, the chief of staff, was sent
by Gates within 60 rods of the British line. Hearing his report, Gates
said, "Order on Morgan to begin the game." Morgan asked to be al-
lowed to move around toward a ridge in the woods, thus outdoing the
enemy's flanking movement. He did this very skilfully. Meanwhile
Poor and Learned, with the New York and New Hampshire troops,
marched straight against the grenadiers under Ackland, and the artillery,
under Williams, was posted on a rising slope. They got in on the flanks
of the grenadiers, and the struggle was desperate. One field-piece was
taken and retaken five times. In a space of 12 to 15 yards square lay
eighteen grenadiers, dead or dying. Ackland was wounded in both legs
and left on the field. This was Poor's attack, as Learned was bearing
toward the centre where were the Germans.

Morgan became effective at the same moment. He crushed Fraser's
flankers like an eggshell, and pressed hard on the right of his line.
Major Dearborn, with two New England regiments, attacking between
Poor and Morgan, firing vigorously, broke Fraser's front. Balcarres rallied these fleeing troops and brought them into action again, under shel-
ter of a fence in the rear. The Americans then attacked Specht with his
300 Germans in the centre. Fraser saw that the centre was being driven

10. Violent wind & rain most of the Night—orders this morng for all to ready to march with 3 Days provisions—Gen! Nixon & Learneds Brigades march about nine oClock, Glovers at Eleven Poors ours at one P. M. as we passed, we found a great number of Horses, dead, Carts & Waggons broke one left with 15 Barrells of powder, Tents & poles some burnt, various other articles Strewed by the way—arrived at Surratoga Sun an Hour & ½ high—found Gen! Schuylers Buildings & the Barracks all on fire, the Enemy on that side the little River—a number of Cannon Shot exchanged, Gen! Fellows [2] prevented them passing the River [3] & to took their Boats loaded

---

[2] John Fellows of Pomfret, Conn., led a regiment of minute men to Boston immediately after Lexington. He was now a brigadier-general of militia.

[3] This stream, called the "little river" on the 11th, was the Fishkill. Schuyler's house was on the east side of the Albany road and south of the river, where the road crosses the stream.

---

and took ground with the 24th regiment westward of the Freeman trilateral of redoubts. He had hardly established his line, when Tim Murphy's bullet gave his mortal wound. The loss of this gallant general disheartened the British, and Ten Broeck's arrival with the New York militia completed the defeat. Burgoyne abandoned his guns, excepting two howitzers, and ordered his troops into the safe ground of the redoubts. According to Hitchcock, the heavy firing began at half-past four; the work was over in fifty-two minutes.

Arnold becomes conspicuous after the retreat into the redoubts, which he attacked at one and another part. He had been removed by Gates, but appeared in the thickest of the fray. His old troops followed him in his reckless charges, sometimes against the orders of their proper commanders. Apparently he was either making mischief or winning victory, without discrimination. It is impossible to decide exactly what he did. Some accounts charge him with intoxication by liquor or opium; certainly his insane passion made him drunk. The inevitable myths of battle have accumulated about his wild doings, in the shades of this memorable evening. There was a tendency, as the years went on, to make his figure whiter and more brilliant at Saratoga, in order to bring with pork—our & Poors Brigade filed off to the left & camped on the heights.

11. This morning a guard was taken from the Enemy consisting of a Surgeon's Mate, Lieut & 36 privates 8 or ten afterward ; some deserters—a moderate canonade & Scattering Musketry all Day—Gen! Poors, Patersons & Learneds Brigades & the Riflemen pass the little River ¹ about half a Mile above the Bridge & extend upon the left flank of the Enemy within about half a Mile of their Lines—

Sunday October 12. A Slow Canonade most of the Day— a Flag sent into the Enemy I suppose demanding a Surrender, Receiv^d Letter from Revd Ward p^r Post from Home & Revd Foster—

13. Wrote Home & to Capt Batchelder p^r Post. The Tents & Baggage came to us this Day—Some Cannonading—28 Prisoners taken—

---

¹ Burgoyne's position was on the north side of the Fishkill, about three quarters of a mile above (i. e., southwestward from) the point where it empties into the Hudson. The Albany road ran between the British and the Hudson. The reader will perceive that this strong column under Poor outflanked Burgoyne and cut off his line of retreat. Our forces had possession of the Battenkill on the 10th. This stream ran into the Hudson on the opposite side, about a mile north of the Fishkill.

---

out his hellish treason at West Point in blacker and more fiendish tints.

Breyman, with his Brunswick men, was holding their right, having a breastwork of rails. Learned drove out the Canadians posted between Breyman and the redoubts. The brave German was killed and the left of his position was surrounded. Virtually the key of the British position was lost. Darkness stopped the Americans, but Burgoyne evacuated before daybreak on the 8th, beginning his hopeless retreat.

I have generally followed the spirited accounts of Stone and Mrs. Walworth. Kingsford, VI., 259, puts the total British loss at 600. Cullum (Nar. and Crit. America, VI., 309) puts the American loss at 50 killed and 150 wounded.

The whole series of movements and encounters, from September 19th to October 7th, are known as the battle of Saratoga. They were the failure of Burgoyne to break his enemy's line, or to beat him in the open

An Account of the Prisoners &c of Oct: 7.

3 Col^{os} one died Since—Sir Francis Clark [1] Aid de Camp to Gen! Burgoyne—Major Sir Thomas Acklin [2] Speaker of the House of Commons—1 Major—Mr Mooney [3] A. Q. M. G.—18 Officers of different ranks—159 Rank & file—100 wounded bro! in—their dead in the field 70—our killed, wounded & missing not exceeding 150—Gen: Frazier [4] died the night following the Battle of the wounds He receiv^d

[1] Sir Francis Carr Clarke, also private secretary to Burgoyne (see Hadden, p. 145), was an excellent officer. According to Wilkinson, Gates argued fiercely with his wounded guest — lying on the general's own bed — on the merits of the American cause. Gates lost temper and in another room asked if Wilkinson "had ever heard so impudent a son of a b—h." Sir Francis was most tenderly treated.

[2] Our diarist mistakes the son for the father. Major John Dyke Ackland, our prisoner, was the son of Sir Thomas. A rough, blunt and gallant soldier, devotedly loved by his charming wife, Lady Harriet Ackland. Much to Burgoyne's astonishment, she demanded a passage through the lines, and took part in her husband's captivity.

[3] John Money, captain in 9th foot, and deputy quartermaster-general.

[4] Simon Fraser, of the Scottish house of Lovatt, was a brigadier-general. Perhaps the best officer under Burgoyne, and there were many good ones in that little army. Brave, energetic, full of resource, he took a conspicuous part in every action. Digby says (Journal, p. 288) "when " Burgoyne saw him fall, he seemed then to feel in the highest degree our "disagreeable situation." His burial, under the enemy's guns, was quite as pathetic as that of Sir John Moore a generation later. Stone (Burgoyne Ballads, p. 290) notices Tim Murphy, one of Morgan's best shots, who killed Fraser. It was said to be by Arnold's especial direction. Murphy was a daring soldier and believed in Benedict Arnold, claiming that he was within five feet of him when the mad Arnold went over the British fortifications at Behmus' Heights.

---

field. Saratoga decided the American Revolution, and is properly classed by Creasy as one of "the fifteen decisive battles of the world."

Gates has been criticized with and without reason. They blamed him for cowardice because he was not at the front in this action. The charges of lack of courage are probably groundless. Often generals

14. This morning Gen: Burgoyne sent in a Frag requesting
     leave to send a field Officer in for a Conference on a
     subject of great Consequence—about ten ºClock
     Major Kingston [1] Adj! Gen: came in & Stayed an
     Hour & half—Gen: Gates offers Terms [2] — no firing
     this Day—fine Day—

15. This Day Spent in Setling Terms of Accommodation.
     The Treaty completed except signing—

16. This morning Gen: Burgoyne sent a Letter to Gen:
     Gates to inform Him that he had been informed He
     had sent off Several detachments from his Army
     whereby the Treated was Violated; & beg that two
     of his Officers might go thro our Camp to Satisfy
     Him; the Gen: assured Him to the contra—after
     many interviews being had both were agreed, the
     Articles signed & they to parade their Arms to-
     morrow at Ten ºClock.

---

[1] Robert Kingston was lieutenant-colonel in the army and chief of staff
under Burgoyne. Since Clerke's death he had been private secretary·
"Appeared to be about forty: he was a well formed, ruddy, handsome
"man, and expatiated with taste on the beautiful scenery of the Hudson's
"river." (Rogers' note, Hadden, p. 63.)

[2] Kingston was blindfolded by Wilkinson after crossing on the sleepers
of the broken bridge across the Fishkill, and conducted into the presence of Gates. He read his communication to the general, who handed
him a paper, saying, " *There, sir, are the terms on which General Burgoyne must surrender.*" Kingston was astonished, and asked that the
general would send the terms by his own officer. He declined, and re-
marked, "*that as he had brought the message, he ought to take back the
answer.*" Kingston made three visits that day.

---

know not what to do next, when bystanders think they are cowardly.
The crowning day at Behmus' was not a pitched battle deliberately
planned by the American general. It was a series of bloody struggles in
woods and blind clearings, developed from the British movements. Our
staff organization has always been wretched, and very likely Gates con-
trolled the action best from a headquarters, where he could be found.
War, after all, is chiefly in the doing. Gates made few mistakes and
profited by the many of Burgoyne. He did the work, and bagged a fine
British army.

17. This is the important Day in Burgoyne & his Army [1] marched out of their Camp with fife & Drum at half past ten, on the flat near the old Fort at Sarratoga, the British Troops locked their Arms, the Germans grounded theirs [2] — Gen: Burgoyne came over at twelve—the began to pass the River about two & continued till near Sunset, our Army paraded by the Road—I went over their Camp, find Lines very Slender, find much mischief done to Guns, Drums &c —counted Cannon Howitzers Mortars a vast number of fine Guns Baggage & Ammunition Waggons, some Tents, Horses & Cattle & many other things—The number of the Enemy who marched out, besides women and Children, five thousand two hundred—the whole was conducted with great Order & decency & out to inspire every Soul with Sincere Gratitude! [3] fair Day, Wrote Home to Rev? Ward p? Waistcot Gen!

---

[1] Digby heads his journal (p. 317), "A day famous in the annals of America." (p. 320) "As to my own feelings, I cannot express them. Tears "(though unmanly) forced their way, and, if alone, I could have burst "to give myself vent. I never shall forget the appearance of their troops "on our marching past them; a dead silence universally reigned through "their numerous columns, and even then, they seemed struck with our situation and dare scarce lift up their eyes to view British troops in "such a situation. I must say their decent behaviour during the time (to "us so greatly fallen) merritted the utmost approbation and praise."

[2] Kingsford, VI., 280, gives the number surrendered by Burgoyne as 4783. The regular returns were not published, but he claims to have drawn these figures from official papers. Compare estimate in the Diary, October 20th.

[3] The articles at first headed "Capitulation" were changed to "Convention" to save Burgoyne's pride. His critics laughed at this euphuism and doggerel verses in London treated the whole American campaign as etiquette.

> "Of Saratoga's dreadful plain —
> "An army ruined — why complain?
> "To pile their arms as they were let,
> "Sure they came off with etiquette.

Glovers & Nixons Brigades moved down a few Miles, ours come over to the C<u>olch</u>

18. This morning the Army order^d order to strike Tents & march down, left the ground at Ten A. M. marched to Stillwater with^t halting, stopped till 4 P. M. movd on Reached half Moon at nine in the Evening, Gen! Glovers Brigade passing the River—ours got over at two—I came down to the point with the Teams.

Sunday October 19. Lodged at half Moon point without Cover—rose at Day break pass the Sprouts, arrived at Albany at Nine ºClock, the Troops pushed on with great dispatch ; & came into the City this forenoon— & encamp on the heights—attended Sermon at Mr Boons's [indistinct] p<u>rd</u> Judges 7 C^h warm & pleasant—

20. This morning Mr Smith, Evans & myself applied to Gen: Gates to have a Sermon on the occasion of the great Success of the Troops—appointed Service to be on Wednesday at 3 ºClock P. M.—obtained an Account of the number of the Prisoners taken by Capitulation the 17th Inst

---

"Cries Burgoyne, ' They may be reliev'd ;
" *That* army still may be retriev'd,
" To see the King if I be let,'
" No, sir ! 'Tis not the etiquette."

It is now known through Shelburne's Revelations that the prime cause of Burgoyne's failure was in the blundering negligence of Germaine, in not promptly sending Howe his orders to coöperate with the expedition from Canada.

England has often undergone greater disasters, but hardly any blow ever more affected her pride. That a fine army of the very best British and German troops should squarely surrender to rebels, — unrecognized, despised, hated rebels, with arms in their hands, — this was something John Bull never contemplated, when he cheerily began taxation without representation.

Viz   British   2442   Gen[s] Burgoyne
         German   2198   Maj Phillips [1]
    Canadian & Tories 1200   Br[d] Hambeton
                    ──────
         Total   5840   M. Reidesel [2]
besides Women & Children which were many—vis·
ited the Hospital with M[r] Plumb found it in good
order, but Scarcity of Surgeons—An Account of the
Ordnance taken in the Nothern department—
            Bennington 5 Cannon
        Fort Schuyler 2   D[o]
          ───── 4 Royals 5 inch
        Beamus's heg[ts] 8 Cannon
taken with the Army at Saratoga   two 24 pounders
                        two 12 D[o]
                        twelve 6 D[o]
                        four 3 D[o]
five Royal Howitzers, two eight inch D[o]
5000 Stand of Arms—large number of Musket Cart-
ridges, travelling Forges Ammunition Waggons—

21. This Day Ensign Ramdy buried with honors of war—
     receiv[d] Letter from M[r] Foster—Wrote Home & to
     Cap[t] Batchelder p[r] Post—Cool & Rainy—

22. Nothing material to Day Cool & windy—visited Hos-
     pital with Mr. Plumb—

23. Settled the Mess account with Col[o] Littlefield & Major
     Lithgow, due to them £5: 14[s]: 8[d]. Gen[l] Poors Bri-
     gade marched down the River—Wrote Home by
     Adjutant Francis.—

24. Col[o] Storer buried with the honors of War—Gen[l] War-

[1] Major-General William Phillips was Burgoyne's second in command
and a member of Parliament. Had had large experience in Europe,
commanding the artillery with distinction at the battle of Minden.

[2] Major-General Baron de Riedesel, of an old and wealthy baronial
family, commanded the German contingent. His beautiful wife shared
his captivity. Her sprightly memoirs have been very popular, affording
the most interesting incidents of the campaign.

ners [1] Brigade of Maletia marched for the Southard
—fair Day—

25. Gen! Learneds Brigade marched, paid M! Shepard
Taylor ten dollars & ¼ & two & half y$\underline{rds}$ of Canvass,
for making my Cloaths &c

Sunday 26. Preached in the presbeterian meeting House in
Albany from Ps. 126, 1, 2, 3. M! Evans p$\underline{rd}$ in the
afternoon—rained all last Night—

27. This Day Gen! Glover set off for Boston with Gen!
Burgoyne & the other Captive Gen$\underline{ls}$ &c—Gen! Gates
granted me leave of absence for three months—obtained a warrant to draw my Ration Money to the
26$\underline{th}$ Inst: receiv$\underline{d}$ of the Paymaster Gen: 159 Dollars
for Rations—drew from the State Store two Shirts
3 Doll & ½ each—one pair of fulled Stockings from
Contin! Store a Doll: & ⅓—Wrote for Major Lithgow to his Brother Cap! Sam! Howard at Boston—
rained all Day—

28. A heavy rain all last Night & this Day—the Troops
ordered into Houses in the City, the Camp being all
afloat.—

29. Rain ceased last Night: began again at 1 ºClock this
afternoon—receiv$\underline{d}$ Six Dollars of M! Hodgson for my
Gun—took a certificate of Col? Trumbal of my pay
receiv$\underline{d}$ to 1 Oct! & Rations to the 26$\underline{th}$

30. Left Albany at ½ past eight   Stop$\underline{d}$ at Mickeles 11
Miles New Eliz$\underline{th}$ton—dined at Hammonds Phillipston
7 miles—reached Duglass's in New Lebanon at half
past five, 8 Miles—roads extreme bad, the Bridges
Carried off by the late delugeing Rain: Cool &
pleasant—

31. Lodged at Duglass's—dined at Parmerleys in Rich-
mond 8 miles—oated at Eastons in Pittsfield 7 miles
—at dusk reached Plumbs in Hertwood 7 miles—Snow
on top of the Mountain—Cool—

[1] Seth Warner, of Bennington, at which place he participated in the
victory over the British. He was an active and vigorous officer.

November 1. Lodged at Plumbs in Washington—Breakfasted at Bushes in Becket—roads extreme bad—dined at Taggets in Blandford—reached Sackets at the foot of the Mountain.

Sunday 2. Lodged at Sackets—breakfasted at Westfield arrived at Revᵈ Lothrops 11 °Clock pʳᵈ for Him P. M. P's: 126. fair Day—

3. Passed the River 9 °Clock dined at Bliss's Wilbraham, overtook Gen! Burgoyne in Palmer; reached Brookfield at Sunset—

4. Lodged at my Mothers—rode in Company with Burgoyne & his Retinue to Worcester—dined there—the Division of Germans in Town—reached Revᵈ Whitneys Northboro at Evening—fair & pleasant—

5. Lodged at Revᵈ Whitney's[1] last Night; reached Mʳ Stone half past Six—

6. Reached Home at 12 °Clock, a N. E Storm—

NOTE.

The diary records the incidents of his life at home until December 31st. It is interleaved in an almanac published by Daniel George at Massachusetts Bay.

The reader will remember that Mr. Hitchcock sent home his journal. Perhaps if that document had been preserved we should have had a more full account of his impressions of the campaign than the diurnal notes have given us.

The following diaries for portions of the years 1779 and 1780 were recorded on ordinary note-books.

Stone's History of Beverly (pp. 275, 276) contains two letters dated at Valley Forge, May 15, 1778, and Camp Greenwich, July 23, 1778, written to his intimate friend, Captain

---

[1] Rev. Peter Whitney, author of a History of Worcester County. Our chaplain had seen service in the half year since he went out from his home a simple minister. Now he came fresh from the triumphs of his companions in arms. And in the same train were King George's generals made captive and escorted by rebel victors.

Josiah Batchelder, Jr., who was in the quartermaster's department. Both letters dwell on the patience of the army under
its sufferings. There are also two letters from West Point
(pp. 277–280) dated July 13 and October 12, 1779. The first
is very gloomy, and we cite: "No period of the controversy
"has appeared to me more critical and alarming than the
"present. The country is asleep, to appearance, totally inat-
"tentive to what ought to be their grand object — defence.
"The currency is on the eve of destruction."

1779

April 7ᵗʰ   Set out this morning early for Camp—The roads
            soon became dry & fine passing—the weather very
            warm—preached on the Sabb. for the Revᵈ Mr.
            Breck [1] Springfield—joined company with Colᵒ Shep-
            ard [2] & Major Cogswell,[3] came thro Westfield, Syms-
            bury &c. joined my Brigade at West Point
17.   Found them in fine health & Spirits—late Learned's
            Brigade here also—put up at headqʳˢ—sent my Horse
            to Dʳ Van Wick's for keeping—cool & windy today—
Sunday 18. This day very cold & high wind—so that we
            could not have service—find the living much more
            comfortable than I expected—sent a line home by
            Dʳ Scott.—

[1] Robert Breck was settled at Springfield in 1736, and there was a
smart controversy over his theological opinions before the parish became
quiet. He was a man of great learning.

[2] William Shepard, colonel 4th Massachusetts regiment, a brave and
efficient officer, who participated in twenty-two engagements during the
Revolution. In the Shays Rebellion he served as brigadier-general and
saved the arsenal at Springfield.

[3] Thomas Cogswell of Haverhill, Mass., was a captain at Bunker Hill,
He was promoted to lieutenant-colonel, 15th Massachusetts regiment.
November 26, 1779.

19. The weather abates some—Intelligence to Day from Gen! McDougal [1] that the Enemy are leaving the east end of long Island & are moving toward N. York—apprehensive yy may attact this place, he orders the works to go on with all dispatch—went up to Forts Putnam [2] & Web—the former appears to be a very strong hold—situated on a high rocky point, over-toped, indeed by some Mountains in the rear difficult of access, but in front not assailable contains a maga-zine finished, two bomb-proofs one completed—a large bomb-proof in fort Arnold a considerable part of it nearly completed—

20. This day the chain [3] was extended across the River; tis secured at each end by large pieres—size is enormous —Wrote home by Mr. Wescot sent two 60 Doll bills weather more comfortable.—

21. This day the Rev! Mr. Mason left the Garrison—I took possession of his Room—D! Thomas brings an account from Philadelphia that several Dutch Vessels had arrived there—his account of high prices from thence exceed any this way & further east—fine Day—

22. This day they began to add to the thickness of the par-apet in the Bastions of Fort Arnold that looks down the River—pleasant weather.—

23. Gen! Orders from Gen! Washington for the whole Army to hold y^{ms} in ye utmost readiness for moving at ye shortest notice—y^t no officer have a chest on any pretence—as the Portmantuas are given them by

---

[1] Alexander McDougall, major-general in the army, was an efficient officer. He superintended the difficult embarkation of the troops after the defeat at Long Island. He took command of the posts on the Hud son March 16, 1778, and with Kosciuszko built the fortifications at the Highlands.

[2] Maps of the Hudson and plans of the fortifications may be consulted Nar. and Crit. America, VI., 451-459.

[3] Nar. and Crit. America, VI., 324.

Congress,[1] high south wind.—receiv^d letter from Major Hull commanding at the lines—

24. Accounts today from Boston of several very valuable Ships taken off Georgia by the continental Frigates.—

Sunday 25. Divine service at eleven oClock, ours & late Learneds [2] Brigades attended pr^d Matt: 6. 33—dined with Col^o Kosciuszko [3] — Col^o Marshall & Capt Greenleaf came to camp, Lieu^t Goodridge & Ensign Shaw—receiv^d Letters from home, the account of 24th confirmed—an exceeding fine day. — baptized child of Richard Northover a Soldier of the Train, by the name of Mary—

26. Pleasant weather—

27. This afternoon I went down to Fort Mongumery in the barge with Col^s Baily & &c—surveyed the ruins of that miserable old Fort, returned to Robinson's Farm, a beautiful house & situation, but much damaged done it by the Virginia^s encamping there last fall, drank Tea with Mr. Dikeman who lives on the farm ; reached home at dusk after a very agreeable tour— fair & pleasant, but somewhat dry.

28. This morning fell a very refreshing shower of rain, about 2 hours long—cleared off fair & pleasant— P. M. went over to see the ruins of fort Constitution tis situated on our Island opposite West point— Capt Marshall's company only upon it.—

29. Major Furnald, Dr Wingate & I went over to Mr Mandevilles & drank Tea—this appears to be a very

---

[1] If Congress had been able to control the abuses of officers' baggage, it might possibly have grappled with the Continental currency.

[2] General Learned was in poor health and obliged to retire from the army.

[3] Tadeuz Kosciuszko, a Polish patriot and one of the most romantic characters of the Revolution. Recommended by Franklin, Washington asked him what he could do. " Try me," was the reply of genius. He planned the encampment at Behmus' Heights, where Gates made his stand, and the fortifications at West Point. The cadets properly showed their gratitude by placing a fine monument there.

agreeable Family; possessed with the polite & more important accomplishments.

30. Violent storm of snow & rain last night, continued till noon—then cleared away, wind continued high the flag staff blew down in the gale—dined with Col? Kosciuszko [1] — sat for miniature portrait —

May 1. May opens fair & pleasant—

Sunday 2. A fine shower this morning—cleared off about 9 °Clock very warm & pleasant—divine service at 11 °Clock Ps : 18. 23.—dined at headquarters.—

3. The Regiments passd muster—drank Tea at Col? Jacson's. [2]

4. In the course of the last night came up a tempest of lightning lasted a considerable time almost incessant —attended with shower of rain—the morning opened fine & pleasant. Accounts from Gen! Mç Dougal's— that a British fleet, destination not known, was stranded on the Coast of France—its contents 7000 men, most perished—the rest fell into the hands of the French.—drank Tea at Col? Mellor's.—

5. Wind very high at N. W. married Sergt Bates and Mrs Lucy Gun [3] —

6. This day observed as a publick fast thro ye united States—divine service at eleven °Clock, the garrison generally out — prd Joshua 7. 13. — dined at head quarters Mr. Mandeville & Family over—news from the southard of Gen! Lincoln's defeating ye enemy & taking 500—very high wind—cool.—

7. Wind continues high at N. W.

8. Pleasant, today.—

---

[1] As indicated above, Chaplain Hitchcock made himself agreeable everywhere. Otherwise he would not have been dining with Kosciuszko, and we shall meet him often at the Mandevilles.

[2] Michael Jackson of Newton, Mass., colonel 8th Massachusetts regiment of the Continental line.

[3] We have had a christening already, and we shall be surprised by the marriages often made by the enlisted men.

Sunday 9. Divine service today at 11 ⁰Clock — pr᷎ᵈ Ps:
119. 165. Dᴿ Hall was here, their Brigade, Poor's
about marching to the westward—Baptized Lydda,
the daughter of George Wilson and Letty his wife, of
Capᵗ Buckland's company, train—wind breazd up
again about noon—baptized, Adaulph, Son of John
Degrove of the above company—

10. Dined at Colᵒ Kosciuszko, went with him Colᵒ Baily [1]
&c to Mᴿ Dickman's, drank Tea—

11. Wrote home by Mᴿ Poland, Colˢ Marshall Kosciuszko
& Meller dined with me this day—very warm &, for
the season, dry.

12. This day Colᵒ Littlefield came to camp—receivᵈ a letter
from home, dated April 30ᵗʰ — it began to rain gently
toward night, continued the evening—

13. Steady rain all night, continued the whole day—

14. Dined with Colᵒ Kosciuszko — fair day — Mᴿ Avery
came here.

15. Wrote home today, by Colᵒ Carlton, to Revᵈ Willard &
Mᴿ Ward—Reports that a large detachment of Transports left N. York very lately, supposed bound to
Georgia—tis said they have taken down a number of
houses in the city—An expedition agsᵗ the western
Indians seems now to be certain, one division to go
by way of the Mohawk River, under command of
Brigᴿ Genᶥ Clinton—another by the Susquahannah,
under command of Brigᴿ Genᶥ Maxwell—a third by
fort Pitt, on the Ohio, under Brigdᴿ Hurd—the whole
to be under command of Genᶥ Sullivan [2] — much is to
be expected from the Zeal & Intrepidity of those
Gallant Officers & the brave & hardy Soldiers who
are selected for the purpose.

[1] John Bailey of Hanover, Mass., colonel 2d Massachusetts regiment,
Continental line. He did good service against Burgoyne, and was a
brave and faithful officer.

[2] John Sullivan of Durham, N. H. Major-general in the army; held
many important commands. This expedition against the Six Nations
was thoroughly successful. Poor's brigade participated.

Sunday 16. Divine service at 11 °Clock Mͬ Avery prᵈ
Jnᵒ 3. 33. fine day—a court of examination sat today
upon the suspected persons broͭ into camp from the
Clove 17 in number, two of the worst having made
their escape — one James Allen who was lately
wounded in the leg with a party of Robbers ¹ who
made their escape, he was left behind & is one of the
above number, says, that they were lately from N.
York & that Genᷧ Clinton & Mͬ Matthews Mayor of
the city, gives every encouragement to their robberies,
rewarding every considerable feat in that way, & that
the Mayor had offered them a large reward to burnt
Governor Clintons & Livingston's houses & take
their persons which they had promised to effect in
two months—he mentions several robberies which
have been committed & by whom, & where some of
the articles were hid in the woods, which have been
found according to his description, which renders his
other accounts more credible—two of them were
hired, by Clinton, to cross the country up to Brant &
Butler to give intelligence, & call upon them to stir
up all the Indians & Tories possible to make whatever inroads they could on the frontiers, & make
their way down as far as possible into the country, in
three divisions all to meet at or near Esopus—to draw
the attention of the people that way, while the Tory
refugees made depredations from York up this way
—O Clinton ² how art thou fallen, from commanding
an Army of Britons, to be the ringleader of a banditti

¹ These were probably " Cowboys," semi-organized British marauders,
who oppressed the region between the two armies. They were opposed
by American bands, who were called "Skinners." The names indicate
the unlovely character of their vocation.

² Sir Henry Clinton succeeded Howe as commander-in-chief of the
British forces in January, 1778. He was not eminent, but few of his com-
rades were. Lord North, remarking on the qualities of the generals they
were sending to this country, said: " I do not know how these names will
"strike the enemy, but they fill me with terror."

of Robbers! His account appears to be fair & honest, & has been found true in several instances— Gen! Washington's conduct seems to be founded on the knowledge of this, in sending three Brigades to the westward ; one in each of those routs.—Another of the robbers was bro! in today, who, said, Allen knew & was with in several robberies—

17. M! Avery return! to Fish Kill—two more persons bro! in today under suspicion — The remainder of Gen! Poors Brigade set out for Eastown via Fish Kill—

18. Gen! Nixons & Huntingtons[1] Brigades ordered to march for Eastown—A report today that the Enemy have landed a party at Hackensack—measured for a pair of boots.—

19. Wrote home & to Esq! Batchelder to send by Post to-morrow—rainy day—drank tea with Col? Kosciuszko.

20. Sent my letters to the post office but the post was gone—an exceeding rainy day—wind S. W. we hear that a boat, in which Cap! Baily & others went down to or near Tarry Town is taken with the hands if not the officers.

21. Rain continued till night—a flag from N. York up at Peeks Kill—bound for Fish Kill—

22. The boat we heard was taken came up, it proved to be another boat with a Lieu! & six men; to whose cap-ture the flag seems to have been accessory—cloudy today but no rain—

Sunday 23. Divine service today at 11 °Clock pr! Job 21. 5. 6, an exceeding fair, pleasant day after a long storm, which makes the face of Nature appear very beautiful—Wrote home N? 5, by Serg! Eaton.

24. Col? Meller & I went over to Mr. Mandeville's in the A. M—dined & spent the day there—extreme warm

---

[1] Brigadier-General Jedediah Huntington of Norwich, Conn., graduated at Harvard in 1763. He was in the court-martial which tried Lee for misconduct at Monmouth.

today.—reports of the Enemies doing mischief at Virginia, particulars not yet learnt—tis said to be done by y⁰ detachment that left N. York, not long since—

25. An exceeding growing season—warm & pleasant—

26. An express last night informs that a considerable party of the Enemy are out & that they have a number of batteaux in Spikingdevil Creek — Dᵣ Wingate & I went up to Fish Kill landing dined with Dᵣ Skinner at Mᵣ Van-Vorough's repeated small showers detained us there till four ᵒClock—set out for the Barracks, reach⁴ them before Sunset—supped & spent the evening at Colᵒ Hays with Mʳˢ Gates—Colᵒ Bedlow, Mᵣ Avery not at home.

27. This day we walked home by Danforths ferry — reach⁴ the point about four ᵒClock—found all hands hard at work to prepare for the reception of the enemy agsᵗ they / do not / come. Lieut Lunt arrived at Camp by whom receiv⁴ letters from home to the 19ᵗʰ inst.—

The infantry ordered up from the lines. Major Hull with three light Companies to be at Chroton River, the others to join their respective Regiments—

The Enemy in their late excursion killed two men near white plains & took several others—about the same time a party near Hackinsack murdered an old man upward of ninety year old—& committed several other instances of barbarity & robbery.—

28. This evening came into camp with a letter of introduction from Esqᵣ Clarke, the Rev⁴ Mᵣ Mᶜ Orkel a Presbeterian clergyman from N. Carolina—he has made application to Dᵣ Mᶜ Water to preside over a new erected Academy in the interior parts of that State—The Dᵣ favors the invitation & the Presbetery are to meet, on the subject of his removal, next Wednesday.—cloudy.—

29. Went round and viewed the works with Mᵣ Mᶜ Orkel, he set on his journey about ten ᵒClock—very warm

today, growing season—orders from Gen! M: Dougal
for all to be on fatigue, to loose no time in preparing
to give the enemy a proper reception if they should
/ not / come.—

Sunday 30.   Wrote home N? 6, by Lieu! Noyes, inclosed to M: Emery—every man on fatigue ergo no
opportunity for service—   At 3 °Clock P. M. I went
over to the people in the read C^hh, a few families attended—as we were going to C^hh met an express from
Gen! M: Dougal, informing that the enemy are
coming up the river in force—we attended service,
Sam! 2. 3, the command! sent orders for all to repair
to their quarters immediately, which we did, found
the men very vigorous in preparing for an attack—
warm day.—

31. Accounts this morning that the enemy are moving up
slowly.[1] Their number of ships, said to be 30 or 40,
tis said also that they have a fleet in the east river—
their army still on white plains, from 5 to 7000, mentioned.—

Some alarm guns fired bet= one & two °Clock those
at King's ferry[2] having fired some hours before, but
were not heard, at the time the enemy's fleet appeared
in Haverstraw bay—the number of guns denote their
fleet to consist of 25 sail the three first to indicate 5
sail & each one after, the sam number, in consequence of this we packed up our spare baggage to
send off—I put on board Col? Littlefield's chest, my
blue coat—three pair stockings—one of silk, 1 black,
1 blue worsterd—my box of notes—one pair shoes, &
plated spurs—1 pair of leather breeches, folded in my
narrow sheet—frequent firing at Kings ferry most of
the afternoon, cannon appear to be heavy.—several

---

[1] This expedition was under Sir Henry Clinton, and its object was to
take Stony and Verplanck's Points.

[2] King's Ferry was below Fort Montgomery and just above Stony
Point.

small showers today—at sun set I was sent for to go on board the Lady Washington Galley to marry— Jnᵒ Thompson & Abia Chase—

Evening—we are just informed that Genˡ Huntington's Brigᵈᵉ has arrivᵈ at Danforth's ferry opposite this point.—The designs of the enemy seem entirely uncertain yet—whether they are to attack this post or do mischief in Conneticut—very warm today.—

June 1.   About 2 ºClock this morning Colº Pattin came into garrison with his regiment from Haverstraw—Major Hull came on early this morning—the block house near Kings ferry, commanded by Capˡ Armstrong is invested—a moderate cannonade began below between 7 & 8 ºClock—continued till near twelve & ceased, from whence we conclude the block house has given up—half past 12—an express just arrivᵈ with dispatches from Genˡ Washington, which left him yesterday—Adjˡ Francis went with them to Genˡ Mᶜ Dougal—Mʳ Francis returnᵈ with an account that Genˡ St Clair [1] was at Pumpton, yesterday noon, with a division of Troops, on his way to our assistance— the block house still stands out, the enemy finding little benefit from firing, ceased—

This afternoon a number of volunteers, Officers & Soldiers went up to the high point of rocks called block house hill & erected a considerable breast work sufficient to contain about 100 men—this a company of maletia came into camp from up river.

2.   Wrote home Nº 7 to Revᵈ Gannett pʳ Post.   This morning accounts are that the enemy have dropt five miles down the river—The reports of this day are various & uncertain—some inhabitants, who have observed from the heights, say there are no vessels this side Tarrytown—others that there is one at Kings

---

[1] Major-General Arthur St. Clair will be remembered as having evacuated Ticonderoga before Gates took command.   He was a man of parts and a skillful officer, though he was not favored by fortune.

ferry—The most probable account of things seems to
be— That the block house capitulated last night on
condition of marching out with the honors of war,
having their baggage wearing their side arms &c—
the enemy had raised a battery against it render any
further opposition useless—that their Troops are
landed at that place & across the river at Haverstraw
—a deserter says 5000 at the former & 1500 at the
latter place—

Gen! Mc Dougall moved quarters to Fish Kill—
Governor Clinton [1] is there with, tis said, 2000 Maletia
—Gen! Parsons's [2] Brigade expected there this night—
Huntington's betwixt here & there Col? Clarke of the
1st Carolina Reg! came in from Paramus, his Reg! en-
camp^d at the Iron works about 8 miles out—pleasant
day—wind at N. W.—

3. This morning things remained quiescent—Col? Clarkes
Reg! came into camp about 11 °Clock—About one
P. M. a Serg! & three, a party of observation, came
from the east side, informed that a heavy collumn
had reach^d the village, about 7 miles from this—between 2 & 3, an express was sent from fort Mongumery, informing that some Galleys & a number of
boats appeared in view—in half an hour a second
came, & says, they are coming on & their number in-
creased continually—

Cap! Soper came up from reconnoitering at King's
ferry, & informs that the enemy's fleet came to
anchor in Peeks Kill bay, their number he thinks is
upward of fifty—an express informs that Gen!
S! Clair was at Pumpton last night—Col? Malcom

---

[1] George Clinton, first governor of the State of New York, served in
that office continuously from 1777 to 1795. No comment on this fact can
make him a more shining mark. He showed great energy, both in civil
and in military capacity.

[2] Samuel Holden Parsons, brigadier and afterwards major general, of
Lyme, Conn., succeeded General Putnam in the command of the
Connecticut line.

goes down to the furnace with the Maletia—Major
Hull commands the light infantry—This evening
Gen! Parsons came to the garrison to take command
—he inform that observers from the other side
say their troops had moved back to Peek's Kill—
Gen! Nixon's Brigade came down near Danforth this
evening to encamp—it is the prevailing opinion that
an attack will be bro! on to morrow morning very
early—with this expectation I desire to commit the
cause to that God who rules over all & is able by the
smallest exertion to vindicate an injured people ; &
who I trust, will make bare his arm for our help—&
shew the enemies of our land & liberties, that the
events of war are in his own hand ; & therefore that
no weapon formed against his C<u>hh</u> & people shall ever
prosper.—

4. The enemie's fleet not in view from fort Mongumery,
this morning—a boat of observation went below &
discovered them near Kings ferry—they continue
thereabout all day, make no movement as we can
learn—they celebrated the Kings birth day by a feude
Joye as usual—the day & fair & pleasant, rather
warm—wind at south—

5. Very little passing today—the enemy lay much in the
same situation they did yesterday—the wind high at
west—the surface of the earth begings to be dry—
Gen! Deportail came to the point this day.—

Sunday 6.   This morning I attended service with the light
infantry on block house hill at 9 °Clock pr<u>d</u> Deut.
31. 6, the men all on fatigue, ergo no opportunity for
service in camp—Lieut Peterson with a party of observation, & others, mentions that the block house is
standing—& there is some appearance of a camp—
but tis said, their transports are mostly gone down
with troops—they are throwing up works on both
sides the river at the ferry—   This evening joined in
marriage Eliphalet Griffin & Joanna Cary—

7. Went over to M! Mandevilles, dined & drank Tea—the enemy much in ye same state—

8. This morning about nine °Clock the garrison was graced by the arrival of his excellency & suit Gen! Mc Dougall &c &c — they reconnoitred the neighboring ground—& in the afternoon return^d headquarters is in Smiths Clove—

9. Wrote home N° 8, & to Revd Willard p^r Post—the enemy have advanced a picquet about a Mile west from the ferry—things remain quiescent—the works go on, but with less vigor—a new work began on the Island—very warm today—

10. A most refreshing rain fell last night attended with some thunder & lightning—the air exceeding clear & pleasant—The enemy remain in the same state they were; tis said they are cutting forage in the neighborhood of their camp, which does not look like tarrying there long—they seem disposed to carry on other than a predatory war at present. — Revd Mr Kirkland [1] came into garrison, on his way to join Gen! Sullivan in the western expedition against the Indians.—

11. Things remain in statu quo—various reports today, of a French fleet on the coast, the affairs at the southard—one says Charlestown is take, another that Gen! Lincoln has beat them &c &c. I shall for the present, set them all down for falshoods—Gen! Paterson came to camp.

12. The enemy chased one of our guard boats—they have a party cuting on the west side, for what purpose we dont learn—a fine growing season—Gen! order for Service at 4 Clock tomorrow & no fatigue.

Sunday 13. This morning it began to rain about eight °Clock

---

[1] Samuel Kirkland of Norwich, Conn., was a pioneer in the Oneida country. He had great influence with the Six Nations and attached the Oneidas to our cause. He founded Hamilton Oneida Academy and its successor, Hamilton College.

dined at Headquarters—just after dinner a letter from
Gen! Green informs that Gen! Lincoln has had an action in which the enemy lost 1480, killed, taken &
wounded—that the account admits of very little
doubt—rain continued most of the day, very plenti-
fully, & ergo no public service.

14.   This afternoon Gen! Washington [1] came into garrison.
The account from the southard is further confirmed
by a letter he has receiv'd from a member of congress
—with some particulars, viz—That the enemy had
reached the lines at Charlstown & made one attempt
to assail them, but were repulsed—were about to attack, the second time, Gen! Lincoln came up with
his body in their rear & routed them with the above
loss—if this be true, & tis tho! there is very little
room to doubt it, I think we may hope for something
further favorable from the situation of that ground—
I dined with Col? Littlefield—repeated showers toward night, 12 deserters came out this day they say
their roll is called every hour in the day ; & that any
soldier caught 300 yards without their guards is
punish'd with 300 stripes without benefit of court
martial—how can they carry on their operations
without confidence in their Troops ?

15.   This morning his excellency receiv'd the following account from the southard,—viz "Copy of handbill
from Baltimore June 9th

Mr Jos White, a gentleman of reputation, this moment
arrived from Edenton N. Carolina & brings the intelligence of the defeat of the British Army from Georgia, before Charlestown S. Carolina which by a rapid
march they had invested about the 19th ult: ; having,
tis said, been encouraged to commit that rash act by

---

[1] The great American was in this season at the most critical point of
his career.   In the light of his final success, we cannot comprehend how
he was humiliated and misunderstood.   Lee's utterance voiced the feelings of the Cabals, "a certain great man is damnably deficient."

their evil counsellors, the tories—The particulars of this great event are gone forward to congress by express, and may be speedily expected—M.ʳ White obtained his information from the hon.ᵇˡᵉ M.ʳ Hughes of Edenton; who just as he left that place, favor.ᵈ him with the perusal of a letter from Charlestown—advising that the enemies forces, supposed to be under the command of Gen.ˡ Provost, consisted of 3700— That they cannonaded the town upwards of three hours to little effect; killing only 2 or 3 of the garrison during the siege, which was suddenly raised by the gallant exertions of Gen.ˡ Moultrie & his troops, who had, to the number of 1500 previously entred the town, aided by Count Pulaski, his corps & a noble band of citizens who have all gain.ᵈ immortal honor— That a sally of volunteers closed the scene before the Town whence the enemy fled with y.ᶜ utmost precipitation, leaving 553 dead on the spot, & did not halt till they had run ten miles—That they had but 2 or 3 Days provision left—& as 4500 had advanced within 15 miles of Charlestown under Gen.ˡ Williamson, & Gen.ˡ Lincoln at the head of 2500 men had entered Jacksonborough on penpon river, 36 miles from that capital & had taken all the enemies baggage, burning the village at the alarm Time for lack of righteous inhabitants; it was generally believ.ᵈ they must fall into his hands—That an insurrection in the Town would have aided their attempt, had it not been prevented by the execution of 40 of the Traitors."
I wish the above account may prove true.

16. This morning opens pleasant.   Wrote home N.ᵒ 9, & to Rev.ᵈ Willard—per Post; the intelligence from southard further confirm.ᵈ but not officially—rainᵈ P. M.

17. Accounts from below that the enemy are taking their baggage on board, look like their leaving that place, Gen.ˡ Parsons drank Tea with me this evening, & gave me the following account of an expedition

against the Indians [1] &c on the back of Virginia.
Col? Clarke of that state penetrated the settlements
back of it reducing the little villages to obedience, &
administring the oath of alegiance to them—he took
several little garrisons, among others Fort Vincent,
left a garrison & proceed on westward, giving protection to the inhabitants mostly French, the Indians
generally fled—while he was carrying conquest some
hundred miles—Governor Hamilton of Fort Detroit,
collected a party of, mostly, Indians—came down to
Vincent /150 miles,/ & retook it—Col? Clarke hearing of it, near 200 miles distant, march? in the month
of February & laid siege to it with a body of men he
had collected from his new subjects with two rounds
a piece; he previously entered a small Village & ordered such of the inhabitants as chose protection
under Britain to move of to them immediately with
their effects, & such as wl? follow him, he would pro-
tect—they unanimously adhered to him—he obtained
a barrel of powder from them—he held the fort besieged by getting under cover of some ground within
small shot of it which look? into the Ambrazure
they had from which they took off the men in
attempting to manage it—He demanded a surrender
of the fort—Hamilton desired three days to determine, expecting a reinforcement; Clarke, aware of
that demanded an immediate surrender or he would
storm and put all to the sword—in the meantime sent
off a detachment, who ambushed & routed them,
killed some & took some Indians who he hung up
immediately in the view of the fort; upon which gave
up himself & garrison which consisted of six officers
and 100 men; who he sent under proper escorts

[1] The operations on the whole western frontier against the Indians
were triumphant.   The camp news was much more trustworthy from this
direction than that which came up from the South.

down to Virginia. Col? Clarke [1] is said to be one of
the most enterprising genius's in the country—& the
above justifies the character.

A large party from the main body came in today, for
fatigue, to be reliev? in one week in one week by the
same number said to be a 1000 ; upward of 200 de-
tached from Nixons Brigade upon the Island [2] to
compleat the works there, to be reliev? in the same
man?

His excellency went up to Fish Kill this evening,
after having spent most of the day in reconnoitring
the neighboring ground, in which he has been inde-
fatigable ever since he came to the point.—

18.   Tis said the enemy's shipping, except one galley, are
dropt down ; & that they have left all the ground but
Stony point, on the west side.

19.   The above report proves false—His excellency left the
point this day for his quarters in the Clove [3] —
M? Avery came on the point to tarry—

Sunday 20.   Gen! M? Dougal came on, to take command
—Gen! Parsons moved over to the east side, his
Brigade pitch? near the red C^hh, No service to day—
men all on fatigue.

further accounts from southard strengthning the
credibility of the former ; but nothing official yet.

---

[1] George Rogers Clarke, a Virginian and settler in Kentucky. His
summons to Hamilton in facsimile may be seen, Nar. and Crit. America,
VI., 727. His career justified Hitchcock's comment. One of the greatest of the capable American pioneers, who grasped the origins of empire
when feeble legislatures and narrow provincial councils cowered at
home.

[2] Constitution Island, often referred to, was opposite West Point,
where the great river sharply twists from south to east and even north-
east to avoid the massive rocky point. The turn makes the eastern
shore, lying in the curve of the main stream. Marshes connect it with
the main land. The famous chain stretched from Fort Clinton to this
island.

[3] Washington's headquarters were at Clove. This post hamlet is in
Dutchess County, about eleven miles southeast from Poughkeepsie.

21. Accounts today from Gen! Huntington that deserters say the enemy have sent all their women down—& are take their cannon on board—

Married Henry Smith & Phebe Cockswain — late Brewer's Reg! —

22. This day I had the pleasure of a long & equally agreeable packet from home p! M! Wescot—Gen! Parsons receivᵈ from Gov! Tryon [1] a handbill, containing a broken account from Georgia of their success in south Carolina—a very feeble support under their misfortunes there—a letter accompanied it inviting Gen! Parsons to embrace this opportunity of returning to their former allegiance to the parent state.—

His excellency came into camp to day, made but little tarry, very warm.—

23. Wrote N° 10 p! Post inclosed to M! Ward Salem very warm to day

24. The society of Free Masons celebrated the feast of S! John [2] — I delivered a discourse to them I Jn⁰ 3. 11—Major Hull delivered a short Oration—a good dinner & some agreeable songs, grand & inspired by his Excellency's presence formed the remaining scene—he receivᵈ a letter from Gen! Green informing that the reason of an official account having not yet arrivᵈ, was; that expresses had been intercepted— but that the fact was true of the defeat of the enemy at the southard, Gen! Heath [3] took command on the east side—

---

[1] William Tryon, an Irishman and colonial governor, was appointed to New York in 1771. England has sent many excellent colonial administrators into all parts of the world. With them have been some of another sort, and Tryon was one of the inferior proconsuls.

[2] Chaplain Smith (Guild's Life, p. 253) records his attendance on this occasion to hear Hitchcock's sermon.

[3] William Heath of Roxbury, Mass., major-general in the Continental line, was distinguished in civil and in military life. Commander of the Ancient and Honorable Artillery, he wrote upon tactics and was useful

25.   Col: Bailey & Tupper [1] dined with us—very warm—

26.   I din.d with Gen! Parsons on roast lamb & green peas—
      receiv.d a card from his excellency to dine with him at
      New-Winsor tomorrow. Wrote home N.º 11 by M.r
      Wescot, sent 300 doll.s — very warm weather.

Sunday 27.   This morning I perform.d service to my Brigade
      in the new Barruck at 9 ºClock from I Cor : 15, 33,—
      went immediately up to Head quarters New Winsor
      —in company with Col: Tupper, Pattin &c—preach.d
      to the Gen! , Family : & guards &c—Job, 27, 5, 6, re-
      turn.d to camp after dinner much fatigued— Tis said
      the enemy are moving down the river—further ac-
      counts from the southard, corroberate former ; but
      none official—a considerable shower on the river
      about 11 ºClock—

28.   The enemy's force is gone down the river—except a
      Galley & some small craft—& 600, 'tis said, on each
      side to keep garrison—whether this movement is a
      decoy, or to make desent other where, or from some
      other cause is not certain.
      The day has been warm, but nothing equall to this
      day 12 months.

29.   His excellency & suit went down to fort Mongumery
      by water — Col.º Hamilton [2] informs me that the
      enemys strength left at their new post, is 800 on this

---

[1] Benjamin Tupper of Stoughton, Mass., was made colonel of 11th
Massachusetts regiment in 1776. Before the close of the war he was
made a brigadier-general.

[2] Alexander Hamilton has been classified by competent authority
among the five men of the first class in Revolutionary times — men who
would have been great in any country and any time. He had been on
Washington's staff since March, 1777. He was his secretary and much
trusted in planning the campaigns.

---

in pursuing the British from Concord. A member of the Committees of
Correspondence and, after the war, of the convention that ratified the
Federal Constitution.

side & 600 on the east—warmer today than yesterday.

This day I receiv⁴ a Certificate sign⁴ by Col? Bostwick,
of forage money due on my account from July 5ᵗʰ
1777 to Sep! 28—from Nov! 1 D? to March 2ⁿᵈ 1778,
—£41 : 8ˢ, N-York currency.

30. Din⁴ at Gen! M° Dougall's ! Warm as yesterday—

July 1. This day I receiv⁴ my wages & subsistence from
Nov! 1, 1778 to March 1, 1779, 500 doll⁹ , by the hand
of P. M. Allen.—

Wrote home N? 12 & to Rev⁴ Willard p! Cap! White—
who together with Cap! Jenkins has resign⁴ . Made a
visit to Gen! Heath. Reports of another successful
action at the southard.

2. Wrote to Rev⁴ Upham & Hilyard by D! Thatcher, reports of further success at the southard—nothing
Authentick—cool & comfortable—

3. Wrote home N? 13, & to M! Herrick, p! Lieu! Chadburn.—

Sunday 4. Divine service in the new barracks at nine
°Clock—Heb : 3, 12, 13, some officers & a few
Soldiers attended—the most on fatigue—at 1 °Clock
thirteen Cannon were discharged from the garrison,
as many from the galley, in celebration of the Anni-
versary of American Indepen°° declare the fourth
July 1776.

Din⁴ with Gen! Parsons—heard M! Baldwin preach at
5 P. M. Exodus 12, 14,—warm day.

5. This day we have account that a party of Continent
troops & some Maletia from the state of Virginia,
surprized & disperse a considerable body of Indians
with some British Troops & Tories who were forming
an expedition against the back parts of that state—
destroyed many of them—took & demolished their
magazine of provisions—& laid waste twenty of their
towns or villages.

this has been warmer than any day this season has produced—M! Baldwin &c din⁴ here.

6.   This M! Avery & I went to Gen! Nixon's dined &
     spent the day, about five ºClock came up a thunder
     shower, rain considerably, some severe lightning—
     one flash struck in Col? Putnam's [1] Reg! — it first
     took a stake about eight feet high, ran into the
     ground under a large rock which it split & ran along
     thro the Tents of Cap! Whipples company—killed
     one man who lay asleep with his head near his gun,
     scorched & wounded about twelve more, one or two
     dangerously, the others slightly,—an alarming provid͏ᵉ
     indeed for poor thoughtless sinners! the unhappy
     victim appeared to have no external wound about
     him.—

7.   Wrote home N? 14, enclosed to M! Ward ; p! Post.—
     Accounts of the enemy burning East Haven & were
     marching for N. Haven.

8.   This afternoon I had a turn of the collick, a disorder
     very brief in camp, the number of our sick encrease
     very fast.

9.   Accounts that the enemy have burnt Fairfield & were
     pursuing to Norwork [2] —
     reports from the southard that the enemy are captured
     there—

10. Wrote home N? 15, p! M! Andrew Thorndike, accounts
     that 4000 troops are on their thro' Horse Neck to join
     impotent Tryon in fulfilling the measure of his ini-
     quities on the Sound.

Sunday 11.   This morning about 9 it began to rain, it en-
     creased & continued all day, attended with a high
     southerly wind,— very cool for the season.—

---

[1] Rufus Putnam of Sutton, Mass., after the war founded Marietta,
Ohio. He was a millwright and then common soldier in the French war.
His ability in throwing up defences at Roxbury impressed Washington.
The General wrote Congress that the millwright was a better engineer
than the experts from France, who were getting appointments. With his
cousin, Israel Putnam, he superintended fortifications at West Point.

[2] This was Tryon's raid into Connecticut.

12. This day has been uncommonly cool for the season—unwell, took an emetick P. M.

13. We hear the enemy have burnt Norwark—A number of Col? Tuppers Officers applied for discharge.—

14. Wrote home N? 16, & to Esq! Batchelder largely on our necessities, p! Post—

   A letter from President Jay to his Father informs that the Islands of Guernsey & Jersey are captured by the French, that Mons! Gerard had announced it in Congress—That Lord O'Conerly at the head of 15000 in the west associated under Lord O'Neal for the defence of the country,—probably a revolt—that Giberalter & port Mahoon are besieged &c—

15. Wrote home N? 17, by L! Goodridge. This morning his Excellency came down from headquarters at N. Winsor by sun rise — and went down the river, return? just at Night—his having been down frequently of late and observing the situation of affairs about Kings ferry—the light infantry being all ordered to join Gen! Wayne [1] by eight °Clock this morning near the furnace—Gen! Nixon's Brigade ordered to march to day but a detachment of 250 only gone—ours ordered to march tomorrow, to be ready to cross the river by five Clock—these circumstances prognosticate some enterprize in view—what it is, will be determined best when executed.—

   A high wind at N. W.—

16. This morning was introduced by the agreeable intelligence of Gen! Wayne and the Infantry having taken Stony point [2] last Night at one Clock by Coup de main.

[1] "Mad Anthony" of Chester County, Penn. The epithet was not fully descriptive, for he was as discreet and cautious as he was brave. A colonel in 1776, he was made a brigadier-general February 21, 1777. Altogether he was a most efficient officer.

[2] Stony Point on the west side and Verplank's Point opposite were at the Narrows, below the Highlands, with King's Ferry between. These

Gen! Wayne's body consisted of seventeen Companies of light troops—about 1200—the attack appears to have been judiciously plan! & as well executed—He possessed himself of the strong fort without fireing a gun; sustained the loss of about 30 killed and wounded—of the enemy 120 were killed & wounded, four of the former, officers—381 and 24 officers taken —in consequence of this important and agreeable intelligence Ours & the remainder of Nixon's Brigade ordered to march immediately—Ours cross! the river A. M. remain! on Nelson's point till towards night when they moved off, and to my great mortification left me behind, being not well eno' to travel, and my horse at Lichfield; I went as far as Mandevilles and, painful as it was, return! back to the point—

17.   This morning I borrowed a horse, to ride to the Brig!. They camp! at the continental Village last night—I found them on some broken ridges within a mile of the enemy's works, which appear very strong—those on Stony point, look formidable. I left the brigade at 5 °Clock to return—met two, 12 pounders, brass, a mile in their rear—after I came away they filed to the right, by the crick; a little cannonade upon them— return! to W. point in the even!; a number of boats gone down the river

Sunday 18.   This day our brigade retired from Vam Planks point up to Continental Village — Clinton on his march with whole army:
Gen! S! Clair's division came on the Point—a number of the wounded bro! up in boats.—

19.   Gen! Howes [1] & Heaths divisions return! to the other side the river.—

---

[1] Major-General Robert Howe was a patriot of North Carolina, previously trained as a soldier in the British service. He was well educated, a good tactician and an engineer.

---

works were planned as outworks of West Point, and were taken by the British in June.

The loss on our side in the late action was 11 killed and 62 wounded—a great quantity of miletary stores brought up from Stony point—the works demolished & the place evacuated.

20. The Brigade return⁴ to the point this day evening—

21. Wrote home N⁰ 18 and to D⁺ Spofford p⁺ Post.   This evening I receiv⁴ the most sensible pleasure by the favor of an agreeable letter from my dear Achsah from July 1ˢᵗ to the 12ᵗʰ and another from Brother Willard of the 6ᵗʰ, by M⁺ Poland.

This day his Excellency removed on to the point—took quarters at the red house.

Gen¹ Waynes orders [1] previous to an attack upon the British garrison on Stoney Point.

The troops will march at   ⁰Clock & move by the right making a short halt at the Creek or Run, next on this side Clements= every Officer and noncommissioned Officer will remain with & be answerable for every man in their platoons—No Soldier to be permitted to quit the ranks, on any pretence whatever, untill a general halt is made, & then to be attended by one of the Officers of the platoon—when the Van of the troops arrive in the rear of the Hill Z, Col⁰ Febeser [2] will form his Reg¹ into a solid Column of half a platoon in front as fast as they can come up—Col⁰ Meigs [3] will form in the rear of Febeser, & Major

---

[1] A splendid military exploit planned by Washington, who instructed Wayne in his own hand.   The orders show how carefully the whole scheme was considered and projected to certain success.   The "short halt at the Creek" probably was an element in the success, insuring exact coöperation.   Wayne's execution was as good as the plan.

[2] Christian Febiger, a Dane, served with marked ability throughout the war.

[3] Return Jonathan Meigs of Middletown, Conn., was an efficient colonel.   After the war he was settled at Marietta, Ohio, and became an Indian agent.   He was known among his clients as "The White Path."

Hull in the rear of Meigs; which will form the right Column—

Col? Butler will form a column on the left of Febeser & Maj? Murphy in his rear—every Officer & Soldier is then to fix a piece of white paper in the most conspicuous part of his Hat or cap to distinguish him from the enemy.—

At the word, *March*, Col? Fleury [1] will take charge of 150 determined & pick? men, properly officered, & with musquets unload? placeing their whole defence on the Bayonet, will move about 20 paces in front of the right Column, by the route N? 1, & enter the sally port, 6, he is to detach an Officer & 20 men a little in front, whose business it will be to secure the Sentries, remove the abbatis & other obstructions for the column to pass thro'.—The column will follow close in the rear with shouldered Arms, under Col? Febeser, with Gen! Wayne in person—When the works are forced, & not before the victorious troops will enter & give the watch word—(*The Fort is our own.*) with repeated & loud voice; & drive the enemy from their works & Guns, which will favor the passage of the whole.

Should the enemy refuse to surrender, or attempt to make their escape by water or otherwise, vigorous measures must be used to force them to the former, and prevent them accomplishing the latter.

Col? Butler will move by the route N? 2, preceded by 100 men with unloaded arms & fixed Bayonets under the command of Major Stewart, [2] who will observe a distance of 20 yards in front of the column, which will

---

[1] Louis Chevalier and Viscount de Fleury, a descendant of the Cardinal, was educated in France as an engineer. Lieutenant-colonel in our army, he was the first to enter the works and struck the British standard with his own hand. Congress voted thanks and a silver medal for his brilliant exploit.

[2] John Stewart, born in Ireland, was Wayne's brother-in-law. Congress awarded him a gold medal for gallantry.

immediately follow under the command of Col? Butler, with shouldered Musquets, & enter the sally ports, C or D,—the officer commanding the above nam^d 100 men, will also detatch a proper officer & 20 men a little in front to remove the obstructions; as soon as they gain the works they are also to give, & continue the watch word will prevent confusion & mistake.

Maj^r Murphy will follow Col? Butler to the first figure *3* when he will divide a little to the right & left & wait the attack on the right, which will be his signal to begin, & to keep up a perpetual & gauling fire, & endeavor to enter between & possess the works, A. A.—

If any soldier presumes to take his Musquet from his shoulder, or attempt to fire, or begins the battle until ordered by his proper officer, he shall be instantly put to death by the officer next him, for the cowerdice or misconduct of one man is not to put the whole into danger or disorder with impunity—After the troops begin to advance to the works, the strictest silence must be observed, & the greatest attention paid to the commands of the officers—As soon as the lines are carried, the Officers of Artillery, with the men under their command, will take possession of the Cannon, to the end the shipping may be secured, & the post at Vamplanks point annoyed as much as possible to facilitate the attack on that quarter.

The Gen! has the fullest confidence in the bravery & fortitude of the Corps he has the pleasure to command; the distinguis^d honor confer^d on every Officer & Soldier, who has been draughted by his Excellency Gen! Washington, the credit of the States they respectively belong to, & their own Reputation, will be such powerful inducments for each man to distinguish himself, that the Gen! can! have the least doubt of a glorious Victory; & further he solemnly engages to reward the first man who enters the works with

500 dollars & immediate promotion, to the second 400, the third 300, the fourth 200 & the fifth 100 dollars, & will represent the conduct of every Officer & Soldier, who distinguishes himself on this occasion in the most favorable point of view to his Excellency who receives the greatest pleasure in rewarding merit.

But should there be any soldier so lost to every feeling, to every sense of honor, as to attempt to retreat one single foot, or shrink from . [missing] . . danger, the officer next him, is immediately to put him to death, that he may no longer disgrace the name of a Soldier, or the corps, or the State, to which he belongs.

As Gen! Wayne is determined to share in the danger of the night, so he wishes to participate in the glory of the day in common with his fellow Soldiers.—

July 15, 1779.   A. Wayne

In the action—of our men—Killed 2 Serg^{ts}, 13 Privates —Wounded 1 Brig! Gen! — 1 Lt Col? — two Cap^{ts}— three Lieut^s — ten Serg^{ts} — four Corporals & 64 privates—

Of the Enemy—Killed 50—Wounded Prisoners 544, twenty eight of whom were Officers.

22.   This day I receiv^d a letter from Mr Garnett, and wrote to him by Cap! Sumner—

23.   The plunder of Stoney point sold, at enormous prices —Wrote to Revd Mr Stone.

24.   Wrote home N° 19 and to Revd Willard,[1] by Capt Whiting, my mare came in from pasture in good flesh.

Sunday 25.   Rain^d all day—ergo no Service—Wrote to the Revd Mr Gad Hitchcock [2] p^r Mr Samson—

26.   A general council of war, held today at headquarters prognosticates some movement, not long first—This

---

[1] Joseph Willard, D. D., LL. D., was settled at Beverly, Mass.   He became president of Harvard College in the following year.

[2] Gad Hitchcock, D. D., was minister at Pembroke, Mass.

day some Coffee, Tea, Chocolate & Sugar arrived
from the State—the only stores they have sent us
since last spring — the last were issued before I
arrived at the point, on the 17th of April—
Very pleasant day after the refreshing rain, yesterday.—

27. This morning I receiv^d from the State Store, for myself
& waiter—10½ ^{lb} Sugar 1^s, 1½ ^{lb} Tea 2 doll. ½ ^{lb}
Chocolate at half a doll per pound—total 5 dollars—
in this country Sugar is sold at 5 doll p^r lb.—Tea at
30 d^o —The difference then, in Tea, is as one to fifteen, and in sugar as one to thirty, which is our loss.—

28. Last night a Sub: & 15 or 18 privates deserted from
Col? de Armong Regiment at Crompond.

29. Rain^d last Night—
Extract from Gen! Orders.

Many & pointed orders have been issued against that
unmeaning & abominable custom of swearing [1] — not-
withstanding which, with much regret, the Gen! ob-
serves it prevails, if possible, more than ever ; his
feelings are continually wounded by the oaths & im-
prications of the Soldiers, whenever he is in hearing
of them—The name of that being, from whose boun-
tiful goodness we are permitted to exist, & enjoy the
comforts of life, is constantly impricated & profaned,
in a manner as wanton as it is shocking—for the sake
therefore, of Religion, decency & order, the Gen!
hopes & trusts, that Officers of every rank, will use
their influence and Authority to check a Vice which
is as unprofitable as it is wicked & Shameful—if Officers would make it an invariable rule to reprimand, &

---

[1] Uncle Tobey's experience in Flanders has been often repeated.   In
our Civil war one of the first and rudest imitations of the contrabands
(escaped slaves) was in trying to swear.   They made wretched work of
it.   No swearing is elegant, but it should flow easily to justify itself, even
from the profane point of view.

if that does not do, to punish Soldiers of this kind, it would not fail of having the desired effect.

30. This month has been rema'bly cool—

31. Dined at Gen! Heath's—not well to day

Sunday August 1.   Receiv^d a card to dine at head quarters —his Excellency and part of his Family attended Divine service with us at 5 °Clock Heb: 1, 13,— several deserters came in—every day produces 5 or six—rain^d in the morning—

2. This day pleasant—

3. Receiv^d a letter from Master Herrick dated July 13, by Sipio—rain^d last Night—

4. Wrote home N° 20—and to Cap! Israel Dodge p^r Post.—

We have various and contradictory accounts from abroad—We hear that we have taken their fleet & army at the eastward—Revington had it that they have taken ours—We have it Count D^e Estaing[1] has got advantage against the British fleet. He, that the British had the advantage of D^e Estaing & taken five of his ships.—The favorable account we are disposed to give the most credit to, from the circumstance of the enemy's drawing within King's Bridge, & fortifying below fort Washington. Cool & pleasant to day.—

5. This day our Brigade was mustered and revew^d — I wrote to Brother Cutler p^r Major Bannister—warm at mid-Day—cool evening.

6. This day there has been some firing heard below, we have not heard the occasion, but suppose it was occasion^d by a body of our light Infantry which had gone down to reconnoitring.—

7. The firing yesterday was from a row-Galley upon some boats of ours,—rain^d last Night & all this day—

---

[1] Charles Henry Theodat Count d'Estaing was Vice Admiral of France, and commanded the squadron, which coöperated with Washington. In 1792 he was guillotined.

Sunday 8. Divine service at 5 °Clock P. M. Exod : 32, **26**, a fine day after the storm.

9. Account today both from Revington's paper and from Philadelphia, confirm former accounts of an action between the two fleets, in which Dᶜ Estaing got the advantage . . . also of our success at Penobscot —particulars not come—

A heavy shower at mid Day—

10. Wrote home Nº 21, to Revᵈ Smith and Cutler, and to the president of the Socy (?) [indistinct] Capᵗ Francis who is going to procure certain Articles of Cloathing —Showery about noon—

11. Rainᵈ all the afternoon—took some Sal : absynthi & Rei—in vinegar.

12. Rain continued all night, warm, fine growing weather —very unwell—took an infusion of sena, manna & Sal : Tart :—

13. This day has been very warm.—

14 Extreme warm to day.

Sunday 15. Divine service at 5 P. M. Mᵗ Avery preached to both brigades, Jnº 17, 3,—not well able to speak myself—receivᵈ a letter friend Plumb, by Dᵗ Young, wrote to him by the same hand.—

Some further accounts of the W. India affair, from Mᵗ Bingham, our Agent at Martineco—by which we learn the action was very severe—great damage was sustained on either side—but that count de. Estaing is triumphant in those seas

16. This is thought to have been the warmest day we have had this season.

by a letter from Genᵗ Lovel, we learn that some of the enemy's outworks are carried—and that they have sunk two of their ships—

The affairs of Sullivan are thought to look doubtful on account of bad provision being sent him.—

17. A fine shower last night—the air cool & pleasant after the extreme heat of yesterday.—

18. Receiv.ᵈ letter from home dated Aug.ᵗ 6ᵗʰ by serg.ᵗ
    Eaton—warm today—

19. This day we receiv.ᵈ six sheeps from Esq.ᵗ Weads
    Canaan, by John—very acceptable indeed

20. This morning I went up to Newburgh with Col.ᵒ Brooks,
    return.ᵈ at evening—rain.ᵈ most of the day, the wind
    and tide against us—ergo not the most agreable
    voyage.

    The following agreable and important intelligence came
    to camp—A. M.—from P. Sterling.—

    That Major Lee with 300 horse and infantry has taken
    the fort on Powle's hook and brought off 150 prison-
    ers, particulars not yet receiv.ᵈ —

21. Rain.ᵈ most of the day, reports this evening that Major
    Lee ¹ was cut off in his retreat—nothing to be de-
    pended on—

Sunday 22.   Divine service at 5, I Jn.ᵒ 5, 4, rain.ᵈ most of the
    night till toward noon, repeated showers all day—a
    very great quantity of rain has fallen in three days
    past.—

    His excellency informs the army, in orders to day, of
    Maj.ᵗ Lee's feat—speaks of it much to his and the
    honor of his officers & men—

    Wrote home N.ᵒ 22 & to brother Willard by Maj.ᵗ
    King.—

23. This day accounts came to camp of a british mail
    taken & carried into Philadelphia—containing some
    important dispatches.

    Also from Gen.ᵗ Sullivan—that he has destroyed an
    Indian Town & laid waste their promising fields.

24. Pleasant to day—

25. Repeated showers to day.—

---

¹ " Light Horse Harry " was a favorite relative of Washington's. He
was most efficient afterwards in Greene's southern campaign. The general said of him : " No man in the southern campaign has equal merit
" with Lee." On this occasion he surprised Paulus Hook (Jersey City)
and took 160 prisoners.

Publications

OF THE

Rhode Island Historical Society.

VOL. VII.   JANUARY, 1900.   NO. 4.

DIARY OF ENOS HITCHCOCK, D. D., (*Concluded*).

EDITED BY

CAPTAIN WILLIAM B. WEEDEN.

Continued from page 194.

(1779, August.)

26. Rain[d] last Night — this long spell of wet weather greatly endangers the health of the troops. Wrote home N[o] 23 & to Rev[d] M[r] Upham p[r] D[r] Adams—dated thro mistake the 27th— Accounts that our fleet is blocked up at Penobscot. cool & comfortable.

27. This day accounts from N. York are, that Arbuthnot [1] is near with his fleet.—
    M[r] Wescot arrived—no letter for me, M[rs] Hitchcock not well.—

28. The fate of our Penobscot expedition & of the fleet, arrived. Tis said Arbuthnot is actually arrived at N. York—

Sunday 29. Divine service at 5 ᵒClock P. M. Acts, 2. 22. His Excellency & suit Gen[ls] Putnam—Heath—Green [2] — Knox [3] & suits — D[r] Shipin [4] Col[o] Cox

---

[1] Marriot Arbuthnot, vice-admiral of the Blue, was in command of the British fleet on the North American station.

[2] Major-General Nathanael Greene of Warwick, R. I., ranked next to Washington in military capacity. His campaign at the South in 1781 brought out generalship equal to any in the war.

[3] Brigadier-General (afterwards Major-General) Henry Knox was born

&c &c— A subject [1] on the tenth Sunday August 29, of christianity might not be amiss—further accounts that Spain has issued a manifesto charging Britain with a 100 articles of perfidy,—and that the French fleet had joined theirs to 75 in number.—

30. Extract from the orders of yesterday—

The command! in chief has the pleasure to announce the following resolutions which the hon^{ble} the Congress have been pleased to pass for the benefit of the Army. The disposition manifested in the resolves is a fresh proof to the army that their country entertain a high sense of their merits & services; & are inclined to confer an hon^{ble} & adequate compensation.

The gen! flatters himself the several states will second the generous views of Congress & take every proper measure to gratify the reasonable expectations of such officers & soldiers as are determined to share the glory of serving their & themselves thro the war, & finishing the task they have so nobly begun.

The flourishing aspect of affairs in Europe & the W. Indies as well as in these States gives us every reason to believe, that this happy period will speedily arrive.

In Congress Aug! 17th Whereas the Army of the United States of America have, by their patriotism, valour & perseverance in the defence of their country, become entitled to the Gratitude as well as the Approbation of their fellow citizens—

Resolved. That it be & it is hereby recommended to

---

[1] A preacher seldom has a better opportunity than this distinguished company afforded. Dr. Hitchcock very modestly records his sense of it, for he speaks of Christianity and not of himself.

---

at Boston of Scotch-Irish stock. He commanded the artillery through the war and was much trusted by Washington.

[4] Probably Dr. William Shippen, a physician of Philadelphia, and a delegate to Congress.

the Several States that have not already adopted
measures for that purpose, to make such further provision for the officers & soldiers enlisted for the war,
to them respectively belonging who shall continue in
service till the establishment of peace, as shall be an
adequate compensation for the many dangers losses
& hardships they have suffered & been exposed to in
the course of the present contest—either by granting
their officers half pay for life & proper rewards to
their soldiers, or in such other way as may appear
most expedient to the legislatures of the several
states.

Resolved.   That it be recommended to the several
states, to make such provision for the widows of such
of their officers & of their soldiers enlisted for the
war, as have died or may die in Service, as shall
secure to them the sweets of that liberty, for the enjoyment of which, their husbands have nobly laid
down their lives.—

Resolved, Aug! 18.—   That, untill the further order of
congress, the Officers of the Army be entitled to receive monthly for their subsistence money the sums
following — viz — each Col? & brig^de Chap^n 500 dollars [1] & all others in proportion — each Soldier 10
doll? p^r month in lieu of those articles of food origi-
nally intend for them & not furnished— An account
of the cloathing due to the men to be made out in
order for payment.—

Receiv^d letters from Revd Ward & Plumb—

31.   Col? Davidson [2] and Dr Burnett dined here—very cool
towards night.

September 1st   West Point.   This intelligence from Philadelphia that an ordnance ship taken from Arbuthnot's
fleet had arrived containing 26 piece of brass ordnance, and other very valuable articles.

---

[1] The fathers appreciated their chaplains well in the matter of pay.

[2] William Davidson, of Rowan County, North Carolina.

2. Wrote home N⁰ 24 by Mʳ Wescot who left the point
about noon—sent 100 dollˢ — Received pʳ post, a
letter from brother Willard dated Augᵗ 23, which informs me of the situation of my family—it came P. M.
I wrote a line and sent it after Mʳ Wescot— Wrote
to Revᵈ Mʳ Ward pʳ Mʳ Whiting.

3. Rainy, dull day.

4. Very little passing—

Sunday 5. Divine service at 5 o'Clock P. M. the Revᵈ
Mʳ Blair [1] preachᵈ for me, from Matt: 7, 12. His
excellency & a large number of gentlemen present.—
cool to-day—

6. Col⁰ Cox A. Q. M. G. observed in company with his excellency & others, that by the calculation of a number
of gentlemen at Philadelphia that the quantity of
currency now in circulation does not amount quite to
143,000,000 dollars, ergo, the depreciation far exceeds
to the quantity.

7. Some accounts from Genˡ Sullivan, that he has had an
engagement with the united force of Butlers [2] Brandt
&c the enemy, they fled and left twelve Indians dead
and all their baggage trinkets &c, which he took, tis
said Genˡ Poor distinguished himself on the occasion.
Accounts from N. York are that an embarkation is
taking place there—how large or where destinᵈ is not
known—
Of the French taking an English 74 and a mast ship in
the W. Indies—

8. Wrote home N⁰ 25 enclosed to Revᵈ Mʳ Willard
pʳ Post.

---

[1] Probably Samuel Blair, D. D., who was chaplain of the Continental
Congress.

[2] Colonel John Butler, a prominent Tory, commanded a regiment of
marauders, traitors and vagabonds dressed like Indians.
Joseph Brandt (Thayandanega) was a Mohawk chief of ability, who
held a colonel's commission from the King. He lived at the head of
Lake Ontario after the war.

9. A shower last night— This day D! Hart [1] & I went over to Gen! Nixon's Brigade return? at evening.

10. Tis said a large embarkation certainly taking place at York—their destination not known, Boston is conjectured by many.

11. This day we had a report that Count d. Estaing has had another successful action near Antego and taken six ships—I wish it may prove true.— very unwell to-day—

Sunday 12. Divine service at ½ past four P. M. I Cor: 15, 19. Cool for the season—a shower last night—

13. This day has been cool—buried a 9. month's man of late Brewers Reg! from Boxford.—

14. This morning I took a powerful cathartic—of Cen ; An-seed, cream Tar: infusion dissolv? in it Man: Glob: Sal: lenctive electuary—to be followed with the heuestis salinis—

15. This afternoon his Excellency, de la Luzerne, [2] Ambassador from the court of Versailles, arrived in camp—his arrival was announced by the discharge of 13 cannon— He has fine personality—his countenance indicates a healthy body & placid mind— appears to be between 40 & 50 years old. This day I have been very unwell.

16. This day I visited a poor, unhappy man of the N. Carolina troops, under Sentence of death for desertion. He appears very ignorant of divine things—but much affected with his state—He was seduced by a fellow of the same Reg! , who has been forging discharges for a number of men, for which crime he ran the gauntlet yesterday & was drum? out of the Camp—& is now in a miserable situation by Danforths, not able to move—

17. The coolness of the weather abates.

---

[1] Probably Levi Hart, D. D., who was minister at Preston, Conn.

[2] Anne César de la Luzerne, a distinguished diplomatist, was minister until 1783. He was much esteemed and beloved by our people.

18. This day I dined at Headquarters—Accounts from Philadelphia that the Spainiards have invested Gibraltar—

The poor fellow of the N. Carolina Brigade pardoned ; some care has been taken of the one who was scourged.

Purchased at the state Store—5¼ lb of sugar at one shilling pr lb.

Sunday 19. Divine Service half past four I Cor : 9-25, his excellency & family present—warm & pleasant.

20. Wrote home N? 26, p.r Sergeant Day of Cap-Ann, pleasant day.

21. This morning the light infantry marched between day & Sunrise toward Stony point—in consequence of reports that the enemy were about evacuating that place—Tis said they have left Van Plunks point—nothing certain from that quarter.

22. No news from below—ergo—conclude the reports of yesterday were groundless.

23. Receiv? a letter from M.rs Hitchcock dated Sep.t 8.th the first after her illness—

24. There are still appearances of a large embarkation at N. York—Tis said they are bound for Ireland, that there is a revolt in that country.

25. Gen! Paterson & Col? Tupper chosen to go to court [1] to represent the state of the army &c &c—

Sunday 26. This day it rain.d — ergo no service—

27. This day fair and pleasant, the coming of Count d. Estaing revived—

28. Wrote home N? 27 by Col? Tupper. Mr. Guild from Coll : arrived on the point—by whom I receiv? a letter from M.r Gannett—fine day.

29. Conducted M.r Guild round to view the works—introduced him to Gen! Washington & family—we dined at headquarters—

30. This morning about 8 °Clock M.r Guild took boat for

[1] The General Court of Massachusetts.

Murderers creek on his way to Philadelphia. accounts the Count d. Estaing was off S. Carolina the 8th inst, bound to Georgia.

October 1. This month comes in fair and pleasant, but very little news.—

The N. Carolina Brigade march^d from the Island via N. Windsor—the light infantry marched from Ca-kerat.—

2. Wrote home N° 28 p^r Capt Walcot—

Sunday 3. Divine Service at 4 changed with Mr Baldwin prd Genl Parson's Brig^{de} Prov : 14, 14.—very warm—

4. The carpenters taken from the works to build boats— Pilots collecting—which encreases our expectation of Count d. Estaing.

5. This day I dined with Genl Putnam—The Lieut Girard came to camp—lowry—raind last night.

6. This day I dined with Friend Baldwin—spent the P. M. at Genl Heath's—cloudy & cold.—

7. Reports to-day of the English being burned at the southard.

8. Wrote home N° 29 & to cousin Phebe by Friend Bald-win sent 200 Dol. Accounts from Sullivan at Wy-oming on his return — his success has answered expectation — He has destroyed 160,000 bushels of corn—forty towns, one of which contained 125 framed houses, besides a number of small Villages—with the loss of less than 40 men including all killed in action, died of their wounds & sickness— Lieut Boyde & 20 men sent out on a party, were surrounded, all killed ; the Lieut & one man, mangled in a most bar-barous man^r — A second freight of Germans, 220, carried into Philadelphia ; the first amounted to 156 & 6 Officers—

This day [1] nine deserters from the Enemy to-day—they say accounts in N. York are that the British fleet at Georgia is taken—also Provost.

[1] Ninth omitted, probably.

Sunday 10. Divine Service at three ºClock P. M.   2 Cor :
    1, 12.   warm & pleasant.—

11. Receivᵈ of Mᵣ Pierce Depᵞ P. M. G. ç61⅓ dollars—My
    Pay and subsistence from March 1ˢᵗ to Sepᵗ 1ˢᵗ—
    Receivᵈ of Mᵣ Knowles for Dᵣ Spafford 237 dollars—

12. Dined at Genⁱ M͜ᶜ Dougalls—A shower at evening
    attended with thunder & Lightning.—

13. Wrote home and to Esqᵣ Batchelder—Nᵒ 30 pᵣ Post :
    fair but windy—

14. This day, fair & cool—

15. This day Colᵒ Freeman & Major Osgood arrived at
    camp ; a committee from the court—

16. The committee opened their commission to the Officers
    of the Line— They made choice of Majors Hull &
    Furnald to join a committee to be appointed from
    court to make a settlement of arrears due to the
    Army.—

Sunday 17.   No service to-day, the men all at exercise—
    Genⁱ. Orders of this day—

" The commander in chief has now the pleasure to con-
gratulate the Army on the Compleat & full success
of Major Genⁱ. Sullivan, and the Troops under his
Command, against the Senecas & other Tribes of the
six Nations—as a just and necessary punishment,—
for their wanton depredations, unparalleled & innum-
erable cruelties, their deafness to all remonstrances
& intreaty, their perseverance in the most horrid
acts of barbarism—Forty of their Towns have been
reduced to ashes—some of them large & commodious
—That of Chenisse alone containing 128 Houses—
Their crops of Corn have been entirely destroyed,
which, by estimation, it is said, would have produced
160,000 bushells, besides a large quantity of Vegitable
of various kinds—their whole country was overrun &
laid waste—& they themselves compelled to place
their own security in a precipitate flight to the British
fortress at Niagara—And the whole of this has been
done with the loss of less than 40 men on our part,

including the killed, wounded & captured, & those who have died natural deaths.—

The Troops employed in that expedition, both Officers & men, thro' the whole of it & in the actions they had with the Enemy, manifested a patience, perseverance & valour, that do them the highest honor.

In the course of it, when there still remained a large extent of the Enemys country to be penetrated, it became necessary to lessen the Issues of provisions to half the usual alowance. In this the Troops acquiesced with most general & cheerful concurrence, being fully determined to surmount every obstacle & to prosecute the enterprise to a compleat & successful issue.

Major Genl. Sullivan, for his great perseverance, & activity, for his order of March, & Attack, & the whole of his dispositions. The Brigadiers & officers of all ranks & the whole of the Soldiery engaged in the expedition, merit the Commander in chiefs warmest Acknowledgment for their important Services upon this occasion

18. A rough calculation of the Arrears due to the Officers of 15 Battallions on supposition their cops were fully as at first — The whole amount of one years pay is   240660   multiplied by

3 is $\underline{\qquad 3}$

721,980   for the three years
     20   — depreciation
$\overline{\qquad\qquad}$
14439600   due as the medium now is—

Dr. Wingate & Capt. Francis came to camp—Receiv'd Letter from Octr. 2nd & from Cousin Phebe—from Revd Cutler dated Sept. 20—

19. Extract from Genl. Orders.
The Commander in chief is happy in the Opportunity of congratulating the Army on our further success— By advice just receiv'd ;

Col? Broadhead [1] with the continental Troops under his command, and a body of Maletia & Volunteers, has penetrated about 180 miles into the Indian country laying on the Aleghana River, burnt ten of the Muney & Seneca Towns in that quarter, containing 165 houses—destroyed all their fields of Corn, computed to comprehend 500 acres; besides large quantities of Vegitables, oblidging the Savages to flee before him with the greatest precipitation, and to leave behind them many skins & other articles of Value.

The only opposition the Savages ventured to give our Troops on the occasion was near Cusuking, about 40 of their warriors, on their way to commit barbarities on our frontiers were met here by Leut Hardin of the 8th Pensilvania Regt at the head of our advanced partys, composed of 23 men of which 8 were of our Friends the Delaware Nation, who immediately attacked the Savages & put them to the rout, with the loss of five killed on the spot & of all their Canoes, Blankets, shirts and provisions, of which, as is usual for them when going into action, they had divested themselves, & also of several arms; two of our men & one of our Delaware Friends were very slightly wounded in the Action; which was the only damage we sustained in the whole enterprize.

The activity, perseverance & firmness which marked the conduct of Col? Broadhead & that of all the Officers of every description in the Expedition do them the highest honor, & their services justly intitle them to the thanks, & to this testimonial of the Genls acknowledgments.

20. Wrote home N? 31, & to Revd Cutler—sent portrait pr Mr Wallis—

21. Dined at headquarters—Just at   Major Lyman come over from Genl Heath with the important intelligence of the evacuation of Stony & Verplank's Points, which took place about midday.

---

[1] David Brodhead, colonel 8th Pennsylvania, was distinguished in several campaigns against the Indians.

22. Took a cathartick infusion of Cena, manna &c very weak and relaxed—

23. Went over the river obtain order for a horse at Danbury—

Sunday 24. Raind A. M. No service—very unwell—

25. A report that Count d, Estaing is in Cheasapeek bay—

26. This day I receiv^d of Capt Porter 121 doll^s the amount of a horse ration account left with Q. M. Francis.—

27. This day I left West Point having obtained leave of absence for the recovery of my health—reached Salem at Night

28. Lodged at Major Bushes last Night, came thro Danbury. Reached Reading.—

29. Lay by at Genl Parsens's extremely fatigued—

30. Mr Guild came on, passed to Fairfield—P. M. I rode to Revd Tenants.

Sunday 31. Delivered a Ser: Job 27, 5, 6. went to Fairfield between meetings—after Service Mr Guild & I proceed to Stratford.

November 1. Arriv^d at N. Haven to dine — put up at Dr Stiles's [1] passed an agreeable afternoon & evening.—

2. We proceed to Weathersfield.

3. Being too much fatigued to go on, Mr Guild left & went on—Revd Marshs lecture Revd Brinsmaid of Washington preached, very cold—

4. This afternoon I proceed with Revd Perry to his house —more comfortable

5. Reach^d Springfield at 3 oClock, dined at Dr Williams put up at Revd Brecks—

6. Arrived at Brother Cutlers at dark—very tired.

Sunday 7. Preached for Revd Ward P. M. Job 27, 5, 6.

8. Proceeded to Revd Whitneys [2] — Northboro —

[1] Ezra Stiles, D. D., LL. D., one of the purest and most gifted men of his time. He was twice president of Yale and a warm friend of Dr. Franklin. He was intimate with our chaplain.

[2] Rev. Peter Whitney, minister at Northborough and author of a history of Worcester County.

9. Reached Revd Parsons's in company with Mes^s Gannett & Guild &c

10. This morning we moved on early to Salem, attended the ordination of Mr Prime. — Arrived home about Sunset after 7 months & three days absence— found my dear Family in health—and thro the great goodness of God my own is much better than when I left camp—may my Gratitude ever rise in proportion to favors receiv^d .

[The above diary fills one note-book. The next note-book begins at August 1, 1780, with the life in camp at West Point. Obviously an intervening book has been lost.]

1780

August 1. Yesterday the N. York, 3^r & 4th Mass^us Brigades left the Point—& marched, some to the Continental Village, others to Peeks Kill—the baggage went down by Water—Tis a late day to take the field but the activity, may make up for the shortness of the Campaign—

The other two Mass^us & Connecticut moved down the evening before— His Excellency is now at Genl Howe's, the main Army are crossing at King's ferry —things at present wear the appearance of a vigorous push, while the British fleet & army are absent [1] —

Col^o Malcom with some York Meletia came on the Point— This morning a fellow was executed as a Spy—he was taken last Saturday, tried on Sabbath day—& executed this morning.—

2. The baggage ordered back — one tent retained for twelve men—

3. The British fleet & army having returned to York, the object of the light & vigorous move ceased—viz the calling their attention from our Allies—the Army directed in Genl orders to recal their baggage, & re-

[1] Clinton projected an expedition to Rhode Island, but proceeded no farther than Huntington Bay, Long Island.

cross the river in order to prosecute the original plan of the campaign—the army to move over the river in Geographical order to begin early to-morrow morning— The Army once more makes a respectable appearance.

4. This morning the light Infantry began to cross at four ⁰Clock—the Pensilvania line followed.

5. The Army continues to pass the river—last evening I receiv⁴ Letters from home & Rev⁴ Cutler by Cap⁴ Story—this day I went up to the point— extreme hot—

Sunday 6. This day I passed at West Point—extreme hot —the heat of yesterday & this day appears as intense as I ever knew it to be—

7. This day I spent in the regions of hospitality, at M⁴ Mandeville's—the heat a little abated a gentle brieze.

8. This morning I left the Friendly dwelling—to rejoin the Army, ¹ which found encamped in a line at Tappond—having passed Kings ferry, thro Haverstraw & Clarkstown, a fine country well settled — this is eighteen miles from the ferry—the people appear to be home bred quite unacquainted with mankind and perfectly astonished at the magnitude of the army, tho' they passed in two or three collumns— The Marquis le F'yatte ² joined from Rhode Island, takes command of the light Infantry.—

9. This morning came on fine showers attended with lightning, from daylight repeated till noon.

10. I rode down to Dobbs's ferry. On the way there is a

¹ The line of march was down the west bank of the Hudson toward New Jersey.

² Marie Jean Paul Roch Yves Gilbert Motier, Marquis de Lafayette, was the romantic hero, the chivalric knight of the Revolution. Our people dearly loved him. Of the highest lineage, with an immense estate, he left his aristocratic bride and his position in the army to volunteer under Washington. Brave, devoted, generous — supplying needy troops out of his pocket — he deserved the gratitude which a nation eagerly gave him.

cavity in the side of a rocky mountain—it appears to be artificial, dug for some kind of mineral—Tis about five feet square and near a hundred feet deep—The country is a fertile soil, but the inhabitants are Dutch. a great vapour arises from this ground which makes it cool towards morning, but tis hot at midday—the land of a red colour—

Sunday 13. The shiping fired a few guns at men on the shore against us—a party ordered on fatigue under Col? Goverung [*indistinct*] at Dobbs's ferry—the extremity of the heat prevented attending worship at midday and miletary exercise at Night—

18. The weather has been extreme hot near three weeks.

Sunday 20. This day at 11 °Clock we attended divine Service the fourth Brigade united with us. I Sam! 2, 3. much cooler than it has been.

21. The provisions of the meat kind fails—I rode out to see Friend Baldwin, & obtained a Dutch dinner of Spieks & apples, boiled—cool & pleasant—

22. No meat to-day again, not a pound for our Brigade. Orders this Evening to march to-morrow—the front to begin at 7 °Clock.

23. The army moved off the ground about 9 °Clock—the dust & heat induced me to leave them at the Church, & go about 2 miles up the road and tarry with Major Bass—

24. I spent the day with him, we go fishing in Hackinsack Creek—his Landlord shot a pike according to their custom in this country—very warm.

25. This morning I set for camp—joined about twelve °Clock at the English Neighborhood (not because there are English here) about ten Miles South of our last encamping ground, in the County of Bergen [1] — I found the Army in a sad state as to provision—having drawn none the day they march'd nor the next till

---

[1] Bergen is the border county of New Jersey, lying behind the palisades. The commissariat was difficult with New York City and the river in the hands of the enemy.

night & then but a trifle, & this day at night a little more—prospects very gloomy on that account—The Light Infantry, & front line of the right wing, are down near Powles hook [1] — some firing that way—

26. This day I rode to river opposite Spikering-devil Creek & to fort Lee—saw the most of York Island, the Sound, long & Straten Islands &c—Two hundred loads of forage brought up, collected by the Enemy —several stacks burnt that could not be got away— Gen! Green Commanded the party below—a Soldier of the Pensilvania line having *ravished a farmers Daughter*, being found guilty of merauding inhabitants, was tried found guilty & executed immediately —others who had aid in otherwise abusing the people were flogged—

Sunday 27. Divine Service at 11 °Clock Rom. 13, 9, 10 the 3ᵈ & 4ᵗʰ Brigades present—warm. Some firing this morning, it appeared to be at Dobbs's ferry, another duel one mortally wounded—

29. Mʳ Evans & I rode to Hackensack a beautiful Village on a small river, where I found Mr. Romaine an agreeable clergyman who, tho Dutch, entertained us very hospitably—very warm—extreme dry—

September 1. A heavy firing yesterday and some this day —the Occasion not known.

2. Gen! Orders to march to-morrow morning at eight °Clock—this has been a lowry day, several small showers—it looks likely to continue—

Sunday 3. Rainy intervals all last Night & this morning —orders not to march till further orders—the rain come on heavy, wind violent at S. E. about ten A. M. continued till two P. M.—cleared off very moderate and pleasant — Mʳ Barlow [2] came to see me — he

---

[1] Now Jersey City.

[2] Joel Barlow, poet and author, born at Redding, Conn., graduated at Yale, 1778, was a chaplain in the army. The epic " Columbiad " did not succeed, as epics seldom have. But he was a good scholar, pure and patriotic, deserving well of posterity.

arrived in camp last Evening to take the Chaplaincy of the 4th Brigade.

4. This day the army retired by the right, the baggage in front, over the new Bridge—left the ground at Tean Neck about 9 °Clock, & encamped about two & half Miles West of the new Bridge. No meat for the Brigade this day—at Steenropia.—

5. Cold to-day for the season— News of Gen! Gates defeat before Cornwallis in South Carolina—No provision of meat to-day—

6. A small supply of beef & mutton for the Brigade—cool for the Season—a heavy shower last Night—

9. Last night departed this life of a putrid fever, Brigadier Gen! Poor, [1] whose uniform life—agreeable deportment — intrepid & determined spirit united to a placid, generous, disposition rendered him at once & equally serviceable to the public and agreeable to his Friends & acquaintance—his death is therefore very greatly lamented by them all—& perhaps no Officer of his rank in the army would receive of more general Tribute than he.

Sunday 10. Divine Service at 10 °Clock—Jer: 2, 19— after service I went to the 4th Brigade & heard Mr Barlow preach for the first time to them, on the omnipresence of God—a very sensible, Judicious Sermon —Acts 17, 28.—

This afternoon were interred the remains of Gen! Poor —the procession began about a Mile from Hackensack Churchyard—The Brigade of Light Infantry he commanded—march in front with Arms reverst— Lees corps of Light horse followed them—a band of musick next—Mr Evans & I preceeded the herse— Brigadier Gen! Bearers—the Officers of the N. Hampshire Brigade followed—His Excellency, the Major Gen^{ls} succeeded—the most of the Officers of the

---

[1] Drake gives the cause of death, "killed in a duel with a French Officer, near Hackensack, N. J., Sept. 8, 1780." A wasteful sacrifice of an excellent life.

Army formed a very long procession—Mr. Evans delivered an Oration at the grave suitable to the solemn occasion—

11. Last Night some Waggoners were attempt to meraude a hog of an inhabitant—he, defending, his property shot the Soldier dead on the spot—

12. This Afternoon was executed at 4 oClock, immediately after sentence—David Hall of the Pensilvania line—for robing an Inhabitant — he with three others blacked themselves & entered the House in the Night, bound the men & made the Women show them where the most valuable Articles were—they made off with their booty—but the Neighbours rallied, pursued & caught this man—& upon conviction was sentenced to suffer death—the Adjt Genl sent a request to me to attend, which I did—found the poor unhappy man somewhat affected with his case, but did not seem to be appear to be acquainted with Religion—

A shower attended with thunder.

As the poor Fellow was going to the place of Execution a number of their women came thro' the Provost to bid him farewell—one seizing him with both her hands, says—"great luck to you David."—

Anecdote— The Troops advanced near Powlers hook, were ordered to march by the Soldier who was taken from the ranks & executed on the 26th August for merauding the Inhabitants—as they passed—one of comerades slaped him on the thigh & says "well Jack you are the best off of any of us—it wont come to your turn to be hanged again this ten years." [1]

13. This morning the whole Army turned out to be reviewed by a number of Indians Some Chiefs, a Committee from several Tribes in Canada—who were sent to Rhode Island to obtain the certainty of a French

[1] Evidently men who had been on very short rations about a month had a fellow-feeling for a marauder. They would bestow on him the best wit they had.

Fleet, which the Briton endeavored to keep a secret from them.

14. This day I obtain more particular Accounts of the Southern affair than before— The British were oblidged to stretch themselves in single file at five feet distance in order occupy the ground opposite to our Maletia, who immediately & run precipetately casting away their guns as usual, this enabled the Enemy to consolidate & turn the left flank of our right wing, regular Troops, the conflict became severe & was tried at the point of the Bayonet fifteen minutes—"when superior bravery overpowered by superior numbers our troops were oblidged to file off which they did in good order." the Enemy's Light horse pursued, about 400—which were almost entirely cut off—tis said only two or three escaped—The Baron de Kalb[1] is dead of his wounds—Governor Caswell of N. Carolina has erected a Camp at the distance of about forty Miles from the Action, has collected about 700 of our Regulars to it—in his letter to Congress he makes no mention of Gates—we lost all our heavy baggage & Artillery— No provision to-day.

Anecdote. An Officer observed that "the Reason why Gen! Gates was so fond of Maletia was because he knew that Regular Troops would lead him into fire but there was no danger of the Maletia doing it."

Sunday 17. This morning his Excellency the Marquis le Fayette & Gen! Knox set out for Hartford to confer with the Count de Rochambeau[2] &c—

Divine Service at 11 °Clock, M! Baldwin preached for me, from Eccl: 12, 13, an excellent Sermon—at 5

---

[1] John Baron De Kalb came over in the vessel with Lafayette. He had been a brigadier-general in the French army and was made major-general in ours.

[2] Jean Baptiste Donatien Vimeur, Count de Rochambeau, marshal of France. As a lieutenant-general with a corps of 6000 men he landed at Rhode Island. The French coöperation was very effective at Yorktown.

P. M. I returned the service by preaching to their Brigade Heb : 3, 12, 13.

18. Gen! Green compliments his Excellency in Orders—by calling on the Army to be very alert lest the enemy should take advantage of the Commander in chiefs absence—

19. Orders to be ready for marching—the unpromising weather prevents it to-day—

20. This day the army moved off the ground about ten °Clock—the baggage preceeded—encamped on the old ground at Orange Town—

22. This morning a firing began at day—occasioned by a Ship & Gally laying Haverstraw Bay—our people came on Tallors point with two & a Howitzer with which they played upon them & caused them to retire.

Sunday 24. At 10 A. M. attended divine Service Heb 3, 12, 13, heard M.r Barlow at ½ past eleven upon worshiping God in Spirit.

25. The whole Army paraded at ten °Clock in two lines and performed the manoeuvre of changing the front—

26. Last night at 12 °Clock Orders came to us to be ready to march at six in the morning — Gen! Wayne marched his Brigade about one—The occasion of this sudden move was the News of a British Officer, said an Adj.t Gen! , being taken on his way from West Point to a Ship below Chroton by three Inhabitants who discovered plans of the works & the state of the Garrison about him—& other papers which detected the Treasonable designs of Gen! Arnold commander of that department, it seems the Post was to be given up to the Enemy this very night—as soon as he heard of the discovery he took to his Barge & was rowed on board the Ship below King's ferry—

Extract from Gen.l Orders — 26 [1]

---

[1] Accounts of the treason of Arnold and of the capture of André may be found in Bancroft, V. 428, and Winsor, *America*, VI. 447. Seldom has any verdict of the time been more fully confirmed by history

" Treason of the blackest dye was yesterday discovered
—Gen! Arnold who commanded at West Point lost
to every Sentiment of honor, of public & private obligations, was about to deliver up that important post
into the hands of the enemy. Such an Event must
have given the American Cause a deadly wound if
not a fatal Stab—happily, the treason has been timely
discovered to prevent the fatal misfortune—the prov-
idential train of circumstances which led to it, affords
the most convincing proof that the liberties of America is the Object of divine protection—At the same
time the Treason is to be regretted, the Gen! cannot
help congratulating the Army on the discovery.
Our Enemies dispair of carrying their point by force,
are practicing every base act to effect by bribery &
corruption what they cannot accomplish in a manly
way. Great honor is due to the American Army that
this is the first instance of treason of the kind, where
many were to be expected from the nature of the dis-
pute—and nothing is so bright an Orniment in the
character of the American Soldier as their having
been proof against all the Arts of an insidious
Enemy—
Arnold has made his escape to the Enemy, but M!
Andrew the Adjutant Gen! of the British Army, who
came out as a Spy to negotiate the Business, is our
prisoner—His Excellency the Commander in Chief
has arrived at West Point from Hartford, & is no

---

than in the case of Benedict Arnold. The only redeeming feature of his
career was his bravery and splendid gallantry under fire. His treason
was not only devilish, it was mean and sordid. He deliberately sold himself and with himself the opportunity which the generous confidence of
Washington had given him. September 25th was to have been the day
for the culmination of the plot between Arnold and Sir Henry Clinton,
the details of which had been arranged by André. Major André had
landed from the British vessel *Vulture*, had held his interview with
Arnold, had been captured and now the chief conspirator had escaped to
the vessel.

doubt taking the proper measures to unravel fully so hellish a plot."—

27. Joseph Smith [1] of Haverstraw confederate with Arnold, was taken at Fish Kill.—

28. This Evening his Excellency returned to Camp to the great Joy of the Army after twelve days absence, a longer term than he has been except in the winter since he took the important command—M.ʳ André the British Adj.ᵗ Gen.ˡ & M.ʳ Smith were brought down under a proper guard.

29. A board of Gen.ˡ Officers [2] set on the trial of André, Smith's refered to Court Martial.

30. M.ʳ Andre found guilty,—to suffer as a Spy—

Sunday October 1. Divine Service at Ten P's: 122, 6, 7, 8, heard M.ʳ Barlow Haggai 2, 9. The Execution of Major Andre appointed at 5 ᵒClock P. M. one Connecticut to attend—a little before the time a flag arrived from Clinton desiring the execution to be postponed till he could send another with some proposals for saving him—the execution deffered for the present.

2. At twelve ᵒClock this day was Executed Major Andre [3] — He received his fate with greater apparent

---

[1] Joshua Hett Smith brought off André from the *Vulture* in a boat. A court could not decide whether he was a dupe or a willing knave.

[2] Greene was president, St. Clair, Lafayette of the French army, Steuben from the staff of Frederic II., Parsons, Clinton, Glover, Knox, Huntington, all sat on the board. If there was knowledge or wisdom in the American army, it was represented on that court and their decision was unanimous. Be it remembered, this was no ordinary treason in conception or execution. The coveted plunder was the citadel of American independence and Major André was adjutant-general of the British army. And yet the pity of it was beyond reason. A refugee and volunteer, the Chevalier de Pontgibaud, testifies in his memoirs that he " can certify that " when they came out of the Court-martial the faces of all our generals " showed marks of the most profound grief; the Marquis de Lafayette " had tears in his eyes."

[3] The muse of history was not so clear-sighted in André's case as in Arnold's. (See Winsor, *America*, VI. 467.) Sentiment did befog

fortitude than others saw it — he appeared a most
Genteel young fellow—handsomely drest in his regi-
mentals—when he came to the Gallows, he said he
well knew his fate but was disappointed in the mode
—He ascended the waggon cheerfully fixed the halter
round his own neck & bound his Eyes—said, smiling,
a few moments would settle the whole—was asked if
he had anything to offer—lifting up the handkerchief
that covered his Eyes, said, Gentlemen, you will all
bear witness that I met my fate like a brave man.

Behold the end of humane greatness! a young fellow
cut off in the midst of the highest prospects, by the
hand of a common hangman—

3.   A cool N. E. Storm
4.   Lowry, unpleasant weather for camp—
5.   The Storm renewed—and more stevere than the 3rd—
6.   Fair & pleasant—Orders for marching to-morrow.—
7.   The Army marched this morning at 9 °Clock—the
     baggage in front—the road very bad—waggons often
     hindered—I went forward to Paramus about a mile
     past the Church — dined at a Dutch Justices on
     Peaches & milk—it began to rain about three P. M.
     the wind rise N. E. which greatly increase the diffi-
     culty of passing—our Brigade baggage arrived a little

---

some historians and even military critics until they maintained that
Washington should not have treated André as a spy, and they blamed
him for injustice. Cooler judgment has gradually convinced to the contrary both English and American writers. The technical claim that
André was protected by a flag is now hardly maintained by any sensible
advocate. Clinton asserted that Arnold's pass and flag should cover and
relieve André. Washington replied that flags must be used in good faith
to justify the bunting or bearer, and that concealment of dress and
papers was the action of a spy. André has been overrated by his admir-
ers. His pluck and graceful manners, his urbanity and coolness did not
change his essential nature, which was shallow. He did not seem to
know just what he was about. He disobeyed instructions in several important particulars. The grace of chivalry is beautiful, but without
honor there can be no grace. The spy may be and sometimes has been
the greatest hero of them all. But the spy must hang.

before Sunset, the storm encreasing—The whole Park Artillery being in front of our collumn detained them till after ten °Clock at Night—when the Troops arrived in fine Spirits, it greatly revived mine which had been depressed with concern for them—many Waggons were left behind—

Sunday 8. This morning opens fair and pleasant—but the scene of yesterday determines we could have no Service.

9. This morning the Army marched at 9 °Clock, baggage in front, to Totawaw, six miles—the march performed with ease, without any difficulty. I viewed the Pesaiack falls—which are very curious—the water runs off into a large crevise in the rocks & falls from fifty to seventy feet—& throws up a great Spray thro which at ten A. M. we discovered a rainbow in compleat circle—there are two clefts—one from one to six feet in width—the other from three Inches to a foot, each of them 70 or 80 feet deep—the sides perfectly parrallel & smooth—

11. I went to see the person at Totowa Bridge, whose head is matter of great Speculation & observation—he lays in a Cradle—is about five long—has no use of any limb except one hand, the other is drawn in—from the chin to the top of his head is 14 Inches—round his over the forehead is 31½ Inches—he speaks with some little difficulty, but appears to have common understanding—is 26 years old—was born a proper child & grew some years—but the head encreased so much faster than any other part as reach its present size—he is free from pain—& seems not unacquainted with enjoyments of animal & rational life.—

Sunday 15. Mr. Barlow & I exchanged Services—Attended theirs at 11 °Clock—Is: 57, 21—ours at 3 P. M.— when Mr. Barlow delivered an excellent discourse upon the Omnipresence of God—Acts 17, 28.—He occupys all Space—Ergo—It may with more propriety be said that all things exist in God than he in them.—

16. Dined at Headquarters—
17. Genl Paterson celebrated the ever memorable 17 Octr 1777, by a large & generous entertainment for all his Officers—where mirth & festivity crowned the day. Capt Greenleaf resigned & left Camp.
18. Mr Wescot arrived with Letters.
19. News of the Capture of 51 sail of East & West Indiaman—in the Channel by the combined fleet.

Sunday 22. Service at 3 P. M. Rom. 14, 17, fair & pleasant.

23. Heard Mr Smith make his defence—
25. I left with Lieut Allen Pay M—Colo Marshalls Regiment, two forage accounts certified by Colo Biddle, [1] one of 522 the other 650 dolls , with an order to draw the money.
26. I put into Capt Porter's hand, Colo Tuppers Regiment, a warrant on the P. M. G. for 6325 dolls received of him 200 dolls to be paid to Lieut Benjn Shaw—

At 10 °Clock his Excellency, the Minister of France and a large retinue reviewed the Army which made a respectable appearance.

News from the Southward by letter to Genl Washington, that the back Counties of N. & S. Carolina turned out spiritedly and charged on a body of the Enemys Levies in the former—killed 135 besides wounded, took 813—1500 stand of arms—also the Georgia Maletia retook Augusta, thinly garrisoned, with a large quantity of stores &c.

27. The Sun eclipsed beginning $^{H.\ M.\ S.}_{10,\ 45,\ 51,}$ greatest obscuration $^{H.\ M.\ S.}_{12,\ 2,\ 58,}$ end at $^{H.\ M.\ S.}_{1,\ 27,\ 11.}$ Duration 2, 41, 21.— tho the Sun was eclipsed more than 11 digits the darkness was not great—it being cloudy, perhaps light reflected from the clouds round the horizon.—
28. Rained most of the day—a change of weather follows an eclipse of the Sun! warm for the season.

Sunday 29. Divine Service at 3 P. M. Jno 7, 46. fair & pleasant.

---

[1] Clement Biddle of Philadelphia, colonel in the army, was an efficient officer in the commissary and quartermaster's departments.

30. This morning left camp in company with Mʳ Lockwood —passᵈ Paramus—7 miles—to Cakaat 10½ miles, dined. go on to Kings ferry 10½ Miles—passᵈ it about sun down put up at Continental Village 8 miles for fear of the Cow Boys who·have infested Crumb-pond of late—

31. We pass the back way by Colᵉ Drakes to Salem 22 Miles—dined at Major Brushes—it began to rain hard at 3 ºClock & detained us.

November 1. This morning presents us with a severe snow storm which forbids our going on—were invited to dine at Esqʳ Hunts—some appearance of an abatement of the storm enduced us to set forward in the afternoon—but it encreased much as we were passing Ridgbury which made it difficult to move ahead—after much struggling with snow, wet & cold we reached Danbury near Sunset—11 Miles—put up at Major Stars.

2. Major Star rode in his Sleigh this morning—at 11 ºClock we move on to Newton 10 Miles—Snow considerable depth on the hills—dined at Baldwins—go on to the new Bridge 4 miles—to Derby Hills 8 Miles—put up at Mʳ Thomlinsons—

3. Passᵈ thro Derby to N. Haven 16 Miles—spent the afternoon & evening in an agreeable circle at the presidents. [1]

4. This day brought us on to Weathersfield.

Sunday 5. This morning we were alarmed about 5 by the appearance of fire below stairs—turned out as soon as possible—found the setting room all in a blaze—with the vigorous application of water it was extinguished, having burnt thro an old Mantle piece & consumed the winscut over the fire place—it destroyed Mʳ Mashes & my hats at the farthest side of the room—attended Worship—prᵈ John 7, 26, Job 27, 6.

[1] At President Stiles's.

LIST OF PROVIDENCE MILITIA-MEN, 1687.

The two documents following — a letter from William Hopkins, of Providence, to Fitz-John Winthrop, of New London, dated April 15, 1687, and a list of soldiers at Providence, prepared by Hopkins and referred to in his letter — are printed from originals recently sent to the chairman of the Committee of Publication, together with several other documents, by Mr. Robert C. Winthrop, Jr., of Boston, with intention that they should be handed over to the Historical Society or the University. They have been presented to the former. The originals were found among the Winthrop Papers. John Winthrop the third (1639–1707), commonly called Fitz-John, and subsequently governor of Connecticut, was in 1687 a member of Governor Andros's Council. As he was experienced and prominent in military affairs (he had served in the Civil War in England), Andros had on January 7, 1687, made him colonel of the militia of Rhode Island and captain of the company in Providence. (See his commission in *Mass. Hist. Soc. Coll.*, 6th series, III. 477.) This early militia list, drawn up for his inspection by Captain William Hopkins, may be compared with the list of persons subject to the poll-tax, drawn up in August, 1688, and printed by Mr. Edward Field in his *Tax Lists of the Town of Providence during the Administration of Sir Edmund Andros and his Council*, pp. 37–40. The names are nearly the same.

[Endorsed : "A list of the Souldiers
at Providence.
Dated April 15ᵗʰ *1687*.]

" for the hand of
Collonel John fits Winthrop
Lieuing at new Lundun —
These with
kare